"YOU'RE A DEAD MAN, SLOCUM!"

Mackay shouted. Slocum ignored him, grinding his knee into the small of the cowboy's back and shoving his face into the ground. Mackay continued to squirm and curse, but the words were muffled by the pressure. His friends started to close on Slocum, but froze as Slocum cocked the Colt and stuck it behind Mackay's right ear.

"Unless you want to see daylight through this man's head come sunup, I think you boys ought to calm down, take this sonofabitch in hand and get him sobered up."

"You bastard," one of them shouted.

Slocum started to get up, and the shouter shrank back a couple of steps. "Think you're tough, don't you, sticking that damn gun in a man's ear. You didn't have it, I'd show you something."

"You were smart, you'd show me your tails, right now."

"Go to hell!"

OTHER BOOKS BY JAKE LOGAN

JAKE LOGAN

NEVADA GUNMEN

BERKLEY BOOKS, NEW YORK

NEVADA GUNMEN

A Berkley Book/published by arrangement with
the author

PRINTING HISTORY
Berkley edition/ November 1990

ISBN: 0-425-12354-5

A BERKLEY BOOK ® TM 757, 375
Berkley Books are published by The Berkley Publishing Group,
200 Madison Avenue, New York, New York 10016.
The name ''BERKLEY'' and the ''B'' logo
are trademarks belonging to Berkley Publishing Corporation.

PRINTED IN THE UNITED STATES OF AMERICA

10 9 8 7 6 5 4 3 2 1

NEVADA GUNMEN

1

Slocum dropped out of the saddle with a groan. He was bone weary and thirsty as a hobo in hell. The Pinon Saloon came highly recommended as the place to go. After three months on the Double Rocker, he thought it was time to see what the town of Dry Spring had to offer in the way of amusement. A card game, poker or faro maybe, might be fun. More fun would be a couple of shots of real whiskey.

Paddy Gibson, the cook for Slocum's outfit, made a passable corn liquor, but just barely. He'd seemed offended when Slocum asked where he could get a real drink, but told him about the Pinon anyway.

So, here he was. A dry man in a strange town. It was the story of his life, so far. He hoped it wouldn't always be true, but he'd been drifting for so long, he sometimes wondered if he'd ever be able to live any other way. Tying his horse on the dry and rickety hitch, he shook some of the trail dust off, just enough to make it obvious he'd tried, and stomped his boots free of dirt on the wooden walk.

The double doors were nicked and chewed at the center edges where they met, even worn and bellied where thousands of calloused hands had pushed them open. When Slocum pushed, the pale oak felt smooth and cold to his touch. The doors swung open easily, their hinges well oiled or often used, and probably both.

The place was well lit, and seemed about half full. Some empty tables formed a half circle around an old upright piano in one corner, but the keys were covered and the stool shoved in. Paddy had said there was a good piano player, but if so, he wasn't on yet.

Slocum walked to the bar, his eyes sweeping the room for a familiar face, or at least a friendly one. He spotted a couple of hands from the Double Rocker and nodded. They nodded back, then resumed their conversation. It was payday, and most of the hands would eventually find their way to the Pinon, but Slocum guessed he was earlier, or thirstier, than most.

He found a place at the bar, shoving the stool aside to rest one boot on the brass rail. The barkeep, a man as round as the barrels he manhandled for a living, wiped his hands on a damp apron and broke off his conversation with two women at the end of the bar. He smiled at Slocum from ten feet away, rolling a bit from side to side as he drew closer.

"What'll it be?"

"What's the best whiskey you have?"

"Well, now, you just might be in luck, partner. Judging by your accent, I'd guess you wouldn't mind a little bourbon, straight from old Mr. James A. Beam hisself. All the way from Kentucky."

"Two," Slocum said. He grinned, and the barkeep returned it, a gold tooth sparkling in the overhead light.

"Right."

The barkeep spun away, light on his feet for so big a man, and snatched at the familiar bottle from a row under a long mirror on the wall behind the bar. Spinning back, he slapped a pair of thick-bottomed shot glasses on the scarred wood and tilted the bottle, backing away to let his professional eye have a better look.

Both glasses brimmed with the amber whiskey, leaving just enough of a lip for a careful man to hoist them without losing a drop. Slocum downed the first in one swallow, then sipped half of the second.

"Been a long time," Slocum said.

"New around here, ain't you?"

"Three months."

"You hire on at the Double Rocker?"

"Yup." Extending a hand, he said, "Name's John Slocum."

"Pete Harney," the barkeep said, grasping the hand and shaking it vigorously. "Welcome to Dry Spring. Where you from, Tennessee, Kentucky?"

"Georgia," and as he said it, he realized just how long ago and far away it was. "Georgia," he said again.

Slocum fished in his pocket for a silver dollar and dropped it on the bar. "That cover it?"

"That'll cover it, and get you one more. First one's on the house."

"Thanks. I hear you have a piano player supposed to be pretty good."

"Must have been Paddy Gibson told you that, right?"

"How'd you know?"

"That's Paddy all over." He glanced at a cuckoo clock high on the wall. "Music won't start for an hour or so. Relax and have some fun. Couple of your outfit already in, and I expect we'll see 'em all before the night's over. Payday's like that."

Slocum nodded, finished his drink, and waited for Pete to pour him a third. This one he picked up to sip off just enough to carry the drink, and ambled over to a table where

Ray Henderson and Danny Page were sitting. The only two men he knew in the saloon, they nodded politely, tilting their hats back as if with a single hand.

"How you doin', Slocum?"

"Alright, I guess."

"Dry Spring ain't much, but it's all we got, 'less you want to ride thirty miles."

"It'll do."

"Hell, ought to be more to life than this," Ray said.

Slocum nodded. "You're right, I guess."

"Ain't no guessing about it. I *know* it. So do you."

Danny grinned at Slocum. "You got to give him a little room. He always gets like this on payday. Turns into some kinda philosopher, soon's he gets a few under his belt."

"No, no, no," Ray said. "You don't understand nothing, Danny. I'm talking about *life*. You know, I mean, what's it for? How come we're here? It sure as hell ain't just to ride around tellin' cows what to do. Christ almighty, there's got to be more than that. Ain't that right, Slocum?"

"I suppose . . . "

"Come on, now, supposing ain't acceptable. What's your life like, if you could make it anything you wanted? Where would you be?"

"Home, I guess."

"Home? Hell, Slocum, tell us about it, don't just throw them words around like that. They don't mean nothing. Where's home?"

Slocum stayed silent for a few seconds. Ray, his head bobbing a little, leaned closer. His breath was evidence, if Slocum needed any, that he'd already had several drinks. Finally, leaning back in his chair to get away from the boozy air, Slocum said, "You guys up for some cards?"

"Hell, yes," Danny said. Taking Slocum's cue, he slapped Henderson on the shoulder. "How 'bout it, cowboy? You ready to drop a little money in my pocket?"

Henderson laughed. "What money? All I got's drinkin' money."

"Like hell," Page said. "Clear the table, Slocum, I'll get us a deck from Harney." He stood up and started toward the bar, looking back over his shoulder at Slocum and Henderson.

As he passed by the nearest table, still looking back over his shoulder, he went down like a felled ox. Danny hit his head on the edge of the table. Slocum saw a burly cowboy pull his foot back, a smirk on his face.

"You see that?" Slocum asked.

"See what?" Henderson was too drunk to have seen anything.

"Bastard tripped Danny."

Slocum got to his feet and walked toward his fallen friend, who was trying to get to his feet. His eyes were glazed, and he looked bewildered. Just as Slocum reached him, the burly cowboy planted a scarred boot in the center of Danny's chest, shoving him back to the floor. Danny grabbed for the table edge, but it was damp, and his fingers slipped off.

"You and your goddamn friends are too noisy," the cowboy said. "Try to keep it down, why don't you?"

Danny tried again to get up, and the cowboy stood, pushing his chair away.

Slocum caught the cowboy by the arm. "Let him up," he hissed.

"Let go of my arm, buddy."

"Let him up," Slocum said again. "Get up, Danny. Go get the cards."

Page scrambled backward like a frightened crab, then hauled himself up at the next table. "Go on," Slocum nodded. "Get the cards."

The cowboy tried to wrench his arm free, but Slocum wouldn't let go. "We don't want any trouble. Just sit down and forget about it."

The cowboy turned, ready to swing, but the look on Slocum's face stopped him cold. "Sonofabitch makes too much noise," he said.

"He's having a little fun. Don't worry about it." Slocum

let go of the arm, and the cowboy instinctively reached up to rub it. Then, realizing what he was about to do, he stopped. Rubbing was an admission that Slocum had hurt him. He couldn't afford that, not in front of his friends.

"Don't ever grab me like that, not ever."

"I hope I don't have to." Slocum waited for the cowboy to sit down. The man glared at him through eyes red rimmed and watery from drinking. Finally, shaking his head, the cowboy sat. Slocum backed toward his own table and sat without looking at the chair. He watched Danny at the bar for a moment, then turned to Henderson. "You know him?"

"Who?"

"Forget it."

Danny gave the table wide berth as he came back with a new deck of cards. The young cowhand sat down and sighed a long breath through clenched lips. "Thanks, Slocum," he said.

"Who was that, you know?"

Danny shook his head. "Won't forget him, though." He popped the seal on the new cards, tilted them out onto the table, and smeared them across the dark wood. "Jokers?"

"No matter," Slocum said.

"Alright, jokers it is, wild of course."

Danny made sure no cards were missing, then shuffled with practiced hands. Slocum watched the drunken cowhand at the next table for the first pass through the deck. He seemed to have forgotten all about them. He put away beer after beer, and after an hour Slocum wondered how he could still sit in his chair. Henderson was raking in the penny-ante pots, and Slocum figured it was time to pay more attention to the cards.

Engrossed in the strategy of draw poker, he didn't notice when a man sat down behind the piano. He didn't notice the first tune, or the second. Not until Henderson had to make a siphon run did it sink in that someone was, in fact, playing the piano. And rather well.

"Guy's alright," Slocum said, as he riffled the cards and waited for Henderson to return. "Paddy was right."

Page laughed. "Paddy said this guy was good, huh?"

"Yeah, he did."

"I wonder why."

"What do you mean?"

"Just look at the bastard, sitting there in them garters. Man ought to know how long his arms are 'fore he buys a shirt, don't you think?"

Slocum glanced over to the corner. His jaw dropped, and he slapped the deck down on the table. The piano player was Paddy Gibson. "No wonder he had so many nice things to say."

Page cackled. "Son of a gun *is* good, ain't he? Should be, his mama was a music teacher back in Pennsylvania. Least that's what he told me. Course, you can't believe a whole lot of what old Paddy tells you. But I'll give him this—he knows just about every damn tune I ever heard."

The surly cowhand was staring at them again. Slocum noticed the man's head bobbing slightly, as if his balance were off. The piglike eyes were glazed with dark pink. But he stayed in his chair, propping himself up with arms folded on the table. He grinned suddenly, and raised a hand to salute Slocum.

The cowboy moved his other arm, teetering slightly. Then Slocum saw the Colt .45 on the table. Slocum got to his feet slowly. He pushed the chair out with his legs.

Then all hell broke loose.

2

The sound of the explosion died away slowly. Slocum, like most of those in the saloon, lay on the floor. He stared at the doorway. The double doors slowly materialized through a thick gray cloud. As he started to his feet, the doors swung open slowly. A pair of boots appeared, high tops, their smooth, polished leather picking up the scattered light from the coal oil lamps and gleaming through the thinning smoke.

There wasn't a sound in the saloon. Slocum's ears still rung, and he shook his head to clear it. Something rattled in his head. It felt as if his ears were full of water, the way they used to when he was a kid climbing out of a creek after a swim. The doors moved, pushing slabs of smoke aside as they swung inward.

Slocum was on his knees when the smoke swirled again, this time with a flourish, as a black and scarlet cape swished through the cloud. The sound of rushing air, distant, half drowned by the ringing in his ears, stopped almost at once as a tall, gaunt figure stepped into the saloon.

Bowing deeply at the waist, the apparition swept the floor with one edge of his cape. Slocum noticed the greasy sawdust clinging to its edge. Marching toward the center of the still-silent saloon, the figure towered over him.

"Good evening, gentlemen," it said. The man, like a black stick with a ball of cotton on one end, shook his shaggy white mane and swept his eyes around the bar. "And, I dare say," he continued, "one or two ladies among you. Women, anyway. I trust I've gotten your attention."

He spun on his heels, waving back toward the door with one bony arm draped in black. "Quite an entrance, even if I do say so myself." He laughed.

Slocum, like the rest of the patrons, was too stunned to react. He looked at Henderson, who seemed mystified, even through his drunken haze. Danny Page shook his head as if he didn't believe what he was seeing.

Slocum got to his feet and backed toward his chair, dropping into it without a sound.

"Go on, gentlemen, go on. Resume your seats." The man waved an arm yet again. "I want you all comfortable. The better to attend to what I have to tell you."

He cleared his throat and waited for the hushed buzz of questions to subside. Wooden chair legs scraped on the floor as most of the men climbed to their feet and took their places at tables and the bar.

"What the hell is going on?" Pete Harney shattered the silence as he stepped out from behind the bar. The beefy barman held a bone-smooth axe handle in one hand as he moved cautiously toward the tall man.

"Are you the proprietor, sir?"

"It's my saloon, yeah. Who the hell are you?"

"All in good time, my good man. All in good time."

"You ain't got much time left, old man, good or bad, 'less you start talkin', and fast."

The old man seemed oblivious of the threatening axe handle bouncing nervously off Harney's palm. He held up a hand for silence, and Harney backed away a step, as if he'd been menaced. He let the axe handle dangle toward the floor, then leaned on it, as if mesmerized.

"May I commend you, sir. Mr. . . . ?"

"Harney," Pete answered in spite of himself. "Pete Harney."

"Aha. Well, sir, I see you have a piano. That must mean you are not without culture, sir. Music soothes the savage breast, does it not?"

Harney, totally confused, said nothing.

"Of course it does, Mr. Harney. Of course it does. I, too, am a man of culture. Much culture. A man of the theater, to be precise."

"We don't have no theater here, old man," one of the cowboys hooted.

"Ah, but you do now, young man. You do now."

"Who the hell are you?"

"I, sir, am Professor Clayton Ramsey. I have done theater proud, striding the boards from San Francisco to the Continent, never missing a step, never dropping a line. I have done Sophocles and Euripides for the crowned heads of Europe. I have done Shakespeare for the denizens of his homeland, Molière for our friends the French. In the original language, I might add, and to no little acclaim, sir."

He shook his head abruptly, and the rising hum of conversation stopped immediately. Ramsey looked away for a moment, then wrapped himself in the cape and strode toward Slocum's table. With a brief wave of his arm, he brushed Slocum aside and stepped on his chair. Then, without missing a beat, he planted one booted foot on the table and climbed up.

"May I demonstrate, Mr. Harney?"

Pete, not knowing what else to do, shook his head.

"Sure, go ahead. But make it quick, will you?"

Ramsey cleared his throat, shaking his head as if something were loose inside it, then took a deep breath. In spite of themselves, the onlookers grew still.

If it were done, when 'tis done, then 'twere well
It were done quickly: if th' assassination
Could trammel up the consequence, and catch,
With his surcease, success; that but this blow
Might be the be-all and the end-all . . .

Harney shook his head in bewilderment and took a seat at Slocum's table. He sat there with his mouth hanging open, not quite believing what he was seeing.

"Shut up, old man." A glass broke, its pieces rattling on a table, and Ramsey stopped abruptly to stare at the source of the racket.

"You, sir, are a boor," he bellowed.

The cowboy, the same one who had tripped Danny an hour before, broke another glass, this time tossing it on the floor right in front of Slocum's feet. "I told you to shut up, old man." He tossed off the rest of a beer and flipped the heavy mug toward Ramsey. The old man ducked away from it, and lost his footing. He nearly fell off the table, and Slocum reached out to grab him.

The bony arm felt like that of a scarecrow, as if there were no flesh at all in the sleeve. Ramsey glanced at Slocum, then tugged his arm free and got to his feet again.

He glared at the cowboy, and resumed, even more histrionically. It was as if he were speaking directly and only to the cowhand.

. . . Here
But here, upon this bank and shoal of time.
We'ld jump the life to come. But in these cases
We still have judgments here—that we but teach
   bloody

Instructions, which being taught return
To plague th'inventor: This even handed justice . . .

Harney leaned toward Slocum. "I don't like the look
of this, Slocum. I think maybe I ought to shut him up.
Mackay's got a wild hair up his ass tonight. I don't want
no trouble—"

A theatrical hiss slashed through the sudden quiet, as if
a giant serpent had slithered in under the swinging doors.
Slocum turned to see a skeletal finger pointing straight at
Harney. "Be quiet, sir. Please, do not interrupt."

Before Harney could respond, Ramsey was off again, this
time railing at the patrons as if they were all as boisterous as
the drunken cowboy.

"You all should know that Shakespeare might do you
some good. Uncultured and unwashed as you are, still, you
are not beyond the Immortal Bard's reach. He can raise you
up, will raise you up, if you lend me your ears."

"Hey, Harney," Mackay shouted, "I come here to drink.
Get him out of here, would you? If you don't, I reckon I'll
have to." Several others joined in, forcing Ramsey to raise
his voice still louder. Tendons stood out in his neck as he
shouted above the uproar. "Beginning in three days' time,
I shall be putting on *Macbeth*. I think perhaps you should
all seriously consider attending."

This time, the drunken cowboy got to his feet, rather
unsteadily, and snatched a mug from a nearby table. He
threw it straight at the old actor's head, but Ramsey saw
it coming and ducked aside.

"Not good enough, my friend," he laughed. "Not half
good enough. You think a fool like you is any match for
the likes of me?"

"Who you calling a fool?"

"You answered the call, young man. Could I have meant
anyone else? Are you calling someone else in here a fool?"

The cowboy was confused, and looked around at the
crowd. "No, I . . . "

"Then I must have meant you, mustn't I?"

"Yeah, I guess . . . "

"There, you see. He admits it." Ramsey appealed to the crowd with a sweeping gesture.

"I didn't admit nothing. You better get down, before I drag you down. Harney . . . "

Pete stood up, leaving the axe handle leaning against the table. He looked up at Ramsey. "You know, Professor, I'm pretty sure we all want to see one of your shows. But maybe this isn't the best place to try to drum up business."

"Nonsense, sir. One must come to the masses if one expects to be heard. Beard the lion in his den, so to speak."

"This is just not a good idea, Professor."

"Don't worry, sir. I can take care of myself." Turning to the crowd again, he said, "Remember, *Macbeth*, three days hence."

Mackay started toward the old man, but Slocum reached out to intercept him. "Why don't you just sit down. He's leaving. Just let him be."

"Mind your own business, Slocum." He reached for his gun, but Slocum was too quick for him, snatching Mackay's wrist and jerking the hand away from the holster.

"Don't do it, Mackay."

He tried to push past Slocum, reaching for the old man's leg, but Ramsey backed away, narrowly eluding the grasping fingers.

Mackay shoved Slocum, who slipped on the sawdust-covered floor and stumbled back into the table. The impact knocked Ramsey over, and he landed heavily on the floor. Mackay kicked viciously at Slocum, missed, and gave the table a shove. It fell to one side as Page and Henderson got to their feet.

Henderson tried to help Ramsey to his feet, but the old man was stunned by the fall, and lay there breathing heavily, his cheek grinding into the gritty floor.

"Maybe you boys ought to take him outside," Harney

said. "I got a business to run here. He's only gonna get hisself hurt."

Henderson nodded. He grabbed Ramsey under the arms and Page grabbed the shiny boots. Together, they lifted the man as easily as if he were a bag of sticks.

Slocum started to get up, but Mackay kicked out at him a second time, and he had to scramble backward, narrowly avoiding the heavy boot.

"That's enough now, Brett," Harney said.

Mackay turned on the bartender. "Mind your own business, Pete. You want our money, you better quit taking sides."

"No need for that, Brett. I just think you ought to let the old man be."

Slocum watched as Page and Henderson pushed through the swinging doors, the old man dangling like a gunnysack between them.

Mackay made a move, but Harney brought the axe handle up. "I'm warning you, Mackay, let it go. I don't need anybody's business that bad. He's out of here, and that's what you wanted. Just forget about it." Turning to the crowd, he shouted, "Drinks on the house."

3

When the doors swung shut, Slocum turned back to his drink and realized it had been knocked off the table. He walked to the bar for a beer, and waited while Pete Harney drew it off, sliced the head with a wooden stick. Harney shoved the beer across the bar with a grin.

"On the house, Slocum."

"What for?"

"Peacemaker. You have no idea how much damage a brawl can do. Mackay's alright, but he has a nasty streak when he's been drinkin'."

Slocum nodded his thanks and moved back to the table.

Paddy Gibson clapped his hands and started pounding the piano keys, but nobody seemed to pay attention. Conversations, mostly low buzzes, broke out around the barroom, as if nobody wanted to be overheard.

Back at his table, Slocum sipped the beer with one eye on the door. Henderson and Page had been gone several minutes before he realized they weren't coming back.

Mackay staggered toward him, a beer mug in one big fist. He spun Henderson's chair around and dropped into the seat across from Slocum. "You think you're some kind of big shot, do you, Slocum?"

"No."

"You picked the wrong boy to mess around with."

"I didn't pick you. You were just there."

"You think so? Let me tell you something. I been here a lot longer than you. Long before you ever signed on with the Double Rocker. And I'll tell you something else. I'll still be here long after you've gone."

"That's probably true."

"What's that mean?"

"Nothing much."

"Nothing much. Nothing much. That's just about right, Slocum. That's just about what you are. Nothing much."

"Look, Mackay, you're a little drunk, and you're not making much sense. Why don't you go home and sober up?"

"Not drunk, just happy, Slocum. Just happy."

Slocum didn't say anything. He sipped his beer, put the mug down, and started to get up. Mackay snaked a thick arm across the table and grabbed Slocum's wrist. "Wait a minute, hoss, I'm not through talking to you."

"But I'm through listening."

"The hell you are." He got to his feet, knocking the chair over backward. It cracked on the floor with the sound of a rifle shot. Everything but the piano stopped. Slocum turned to look at Paddy, who was watching him over one shoulder, his hands still working the keys. Paddy shook his head, and Slocum got the point. Mackay was not somebody to mess with. Not in his current frame of mind, anyway.

Slocum jerked free and started toward the door.

"Where the hell do you think you're going?" Mackay shouted.

"Home," Slocum said.

As Mackay rounded the table, Slocum squared to meet him. Mackay's first punch sailed past his head, and Slocum grabbed the arm, jerking Mackay off balance. Ignoring the stench of the whiskey, he leaned in to the cowhand. "Look, Mackay, I got no quarrel with you. I don't want to fight, and I won't, unless you leave me no choice. In your current state, I wouldn't recommend that. Just let it be."

He shoved Mackay away, and the cowboy tripped over his own feet and landed on his butt on the floor. Slocum nodded toward Pete Harney, who came out from behind the bar, the axe handle once again prominently displayed in his right fist.

Slocum backed toward the door, keeping an eye on Mackay all the way. Behind him, he was conscious of the crowd parting to let him through.

When his back hit the doors, he shoved them aside with his elbows and let them swing shut.

Outside, he noticed that Henderson and Page were long gone. Their horses no longer stood next to his own at the hitching post. He stepped into the dusty street and reached for his reins, when he heard a groan somewhere in the shadows. He froze for a moment, waiting for the sound to be repeated. When it wasn't, he shrugged and started to pull the reins free.

Swinging into the saddle, he heard it again. He stopped and listened. For a minute, all he heard was the creak of leather under him. Then it came again, a low moan, a few mumbled words, all but unintelligible.

Slocum dropped out of the saddle again and flipped the reins around the hitch, letting their weight loop around the post loosely. He walked toward the corner of the saloon, where a narrow alley led to the rear. He stood with one hand on his gun butt, straining his ears. Another moan, this one much closer, and he knew he had to see what was going on.

Stepping into the shadows, he squinted into the recesses of the alley. Moving cautiously, one step at a time, he nearly stumbled over something lying against the wall. He reached out with a toe and felt a clump of shadow yield to his touch. Dropping to one knee, he reached for a match, striking it on the heel of his boot. In the sudden glare, he recognized Clayton Ramsey.

He shook the old man by the shoulder, but Ramsey didn't respond. Getting down on both knees, he pulled the old actor up and propped him against the wooden wall of the saloon. Ramsey moaned again, and Slocum said, "Professor Ramsey, can you hear me?"

Ramsey groaned, for the first time moving on his own. He raised a hand to his head and covered his brow with bony fingers. "My head," he mumbled. "My head hurts."

"Can you stand up?"

"I don't know."

"Try . . ."

Ramsey let the hand fall away, and Slocum heard him move, trying to unfold his limbs in order to stand. Getting to his feet, Slocum reached down into the shadows, groping for Ramsey's hand, but the old man shrugged him off. He hauled himself to his feet, leaning against the wall for support.

"Are you alright?" Slocum asked.

"I think so."

"Can you walk?"

"Not sure." All the bombast of his entrance to the saloon was gone. The powerful voice was reduced to a frail, almost pathetic whisper. "Thank you, young man," he said.

Taking a step, he kept one hand on the wall behind him. It was difficult to see him, the black clothing blending with the darkness in the alley, letting his pale face float like an apparition six feet off the ground.

"Okay?" Slocum asked.

"So far, son, so far."

He took another tentative step, still keeping one hand on the wall. Slocum saw the flattened hand like a smear of gray on the wood. Then it moved away, carefully, almost reluctantly, and Ramsey took another step. Slocum backed away from him, like an anxious father coaxing a child's first steps.

Ramsey seemed to totter on his spindly legs, but managed another three steps before losing his balance and falling to the ground. The old man groaned and Slocum bent to haul him up again. "You better let me help you, Professor. Where do you want to go?"

"I am perfectly capable of fending for myself, young man."

"Doesn't look like it to me, Professor."

"Appearances can be deceiving, young man. They often are. I have managed for sixty years and more. I see no reason why I can't continue to manage."

"You took a pretty good spill in there. You hit your head pretty hard."

"I have taken worse spills and many of them, son."

"I'd feel better, all the same, if you'd let me help you."

"Very well, if your conscience is bothering you, I suppose it can't hurt."

"My conscience is fine."

"Then you are that rarest of men, son."

"What is that?"

"A good man."

"Not so rare."

"Reach my age before you contradict me, Mr. . . . ."

"Slocum, John Slocum."

"I have seen things you've never dreamed of, Mr. Slocum, good and bad. And the bad is worse than you can imagine."

Slocum grunted. He couldn't imagine anything worse than Stone Mountain or Shiloh, and he didn't even want to try. But there was no point in arguing with a half-crazy old man. He kept one hand under Ramsey's left arm and held him upright while the old actor tried placing one foot in front of the other. After a dozen steps, they were near the mouth of the alley. In the dim light it was possible to see that Ramsey had taken a sharp blow to the head. A trickle of blood had dried on one cheek, smeared by fingertips into a dark brown map across the sunken landscape.

Slocum had to take more of the old man's weight as they moved into the street. He tried to get Ramsey up onto the walk, but Ramsey refused.

"I am quite alright. I'll just toddle along home, now."

"You sure?"

"Yes, I'm . . . "

"My God, what have you done to him?" It was a woman's voice, and Slocum, startled, spun around to see who had spoken. "Leave him alone," she shrieked. "Leave him alone. . . . "

She came running up the street, and Slocum was nearly knocked over as she ripped the old man from his grasp. "Are you alright?" she said. Her voice was near breaking, and her hands fluttered around Ramsey's face like frightened birds.

"Ma'am, I think he'll be alright. He just—"

The blow caught him by surprise. She swung from the heels, connecting with an open palm against his unprotected cheek.

"You bastard," she shouted. "What did he ever do to you?"

Slocum brought a hand up to his cheek, which felt as if it were on fire. "Ma'am, I just—"

"You nothing. You just nothing. Go away and leave us alone."

"I was just trying to help, that's all."

"You've done a fine job of it, beating a defenseless old man."

"I didn't beat anyone. He—"

"Liar. You're a coward and a liar too. Go away!"

There was no arguing with her. Fiercely, she yanked on Ramsey's arm, and he nearly fell as she pulled him off balance. Jerking him upright again, she started back down the street. "I told you, but you wouldn't listen. How many times have I told you? Why can't you learn?" She continued the tirade as they disappeared into the shadows toward the far end of the street.

Slocum, still stunned by the onslaught, stood for a moment, watching them. A sudden flash of lightning threw them into sharp relief against the dusty street. The sky split open with a tremendous clap of thunder, and it started to pour. A cold, slashing rain swept in sheets across the street. Slocum started to run, catching up to Ramsey and the woman as the wind picked up.

She wheeled on him as he took the old man's shoulder. "What do you want? Can't you just leave him alone?"

"Look, let me help you. He doesn't need to get soaked on top of everything else."

She looked skeptical, but he started to move, taking most of Ramsey's weight, and she relented. Together, they stumbled down the street, their feet slipping on the slickening clay. Already, puddles had started to collect in the rutted surface. Slocum's feet almost went out from under him once, and he staggered for two or three steps before regaining his balance.

The woman kept glaring at him, but she said nothing. Ramsey sagged between them, his feet barely moving as they hurried him along. He moaned once or twice, but seemed conscious.

Slocum was already drenched, and Ramsey, too, was soaked to the skin. The woman looked like a drowned rat, but she didn't seem to care about appearances. She kept leaning in toward the old actor, as if she wanted to say something without being overheard. But her lips never moved.

At the far end of the street, another flash of lightning gave him a glimpse of several wagons, apparently their destination. She steered them toward the wagon on the left, trying to hurry now, as they drew close. Slocum held the old man up as she mounted steps to the rear of the wagon.

She leaned down and took Ramsey by both arms. "Come on, Daddy, you can make it," she whispered. Ramsey fumbled up the first step, and Slocum climbed after him, still holding most of Ramsey's weight. Two more steps, and the woman backed through a blanket hung like a curtain across the wagon's rear. Ramsey stumbled through after her.

Slocum stood for a long moment, waiting on the steps. But the woman never reappeared. When he started to realize she wasn't going to, he shrugged. He dropped to the mud and backed away, still thinking she might come back.

Finally, convinced he'd seen the last of her, he turned and walked away, his feet slipping on the slick skin of the clay. He glanced once over his shoulder, but nothing moved. A dim light seeped out around the edges of the blanket.

By the time he glanced back a second time, the light, too, was gone.

4

The rain came down even harder, and Slocum wasn't in the mood for the long, uncomfortable ride back to the Double Rocker. Dry Spring had two hotels, neither of which was going to threaten civilization in any serious way, but either of them beat the soggy ride back to the ranch. He wanted a drink, but there was no way in hell he wanted another tangle with Brett Mackay. The big cowboy was one of those bullheaded bastards who could manage to think of only one thing at a time. It was just Slocum's luck that, tonight, he seemed to be on Mackay's mind.

He crossed the street, his boots slogging through the shallow puddles already rippling on the baked clay. Here and there he slipped as the water-softened surface gave way under his tread. Clumps of gooey clay stuck to his boots, making the footing even more treacherous. The Dry Spring Hotel was a block away, at the far edge of town, but of the two choices, it had the better reputation. If he was lucky, and there was no reason to think he would be, there might be a vacant room.

Passing Harney's place, he felt guilty about leaving the horse out, then decided he'd better get a room for himself or they'd both end up sleeping on the street. He could try the livery stable later, once he was sure he'd be staying in town.

The hotel was only dimly lit, but the front door was open and a clerk dozed behind the big walnut front desk. He waited patiently, conscious of the water running off his clothes and leaving small muddy puddles on the blue carpet. Clearing his throat with unnecessary energy, he still failed to wake the clerk. Finally, he rapped the bell, and the clerk snapped his head up, trying to look as if he'd been awake the whole time.

"Yes sir, what can I do for you?"

"Got a room available?"

"Yes sir, sure do."

"How much?"

"Single or double bed?"

"Single's fine."

The clerk winked. "You sure, pardner?"

Slocum sighed. "Yes, I'm sure."

"Alright, then. Two dollars."

"Kind of steep, isn't it?"

"You want class, you have to pay for it, mister."

"I wanted class, I'd have gone to Cheyenne."

The clerk tried hard to pout. It only looked silly. "That wasn't necessary. We run a nice place here."

"Look, I'm tired, and I want a room. You gonna rent me one, or not?"

"Of course, sir, of course I am. Sign the register, would you please?" He spun the thick book around on a hidden lazy Susan, offering Slocum a thick-nibbed pen after jabbing it into an inkpot.

Slocum snatched at the pen and scribbled his name with a rasp of metal on the thick paper. He set the pen in the ledger, closed it, and spun it back toward the clerk. "Key?" he asked, extending an open palm.

The clerk turned to a bank of pigeonholes, most of which were empty, and snared a key on a fancy key ring. He slapped it in Slocum's hand. "Second floor, turn left. Last room on the right. Can I get you anything else?"

"No, thanks. You have any idea what time the livery stable's open until?"

Ostentatiously, the clerk pulled a pocket watch into view and pressed the spring-loaded latch. It popped open and the clerk nodded. "You got about twenty minutes."

Slocum grunted and started toward the door.

"The key," the clerk snapped.

Slocum stopped in his tracks. "You say something?"

"The key. House rule. You leave the key right here at the desk when you're not in your room."

"I'll be right back."

"Makes no difference. You got to leave the key."

Slocum tossed it to him, watching the close-set eyes widen as the heavy metal sailed toward his head. He ducked, and the key slammed into the pigeonholes, then clattered to the floor.

"Didn't have to do that."

"Thought you'd catch it," Slocum grinned.

The clerk was not amused. Slocum turned back toward the door. Outside, it was raining harder than ever. He stood under the hotel marquee for a few moments, hoping it would let up. But he only had twenty minutes to get the horse squared away. He wished he had his slicker, but it was wrapped around his bedroll. It struck him funny that it was keeping dry blankets he wouldn't be using, and he'd have to get drenched for the second time to get it in out of the rain. Some days, he thought, it just doesn't pay to get up.

Shaking his head, he stepped out from under the protective cover and into the downpour. The puddles, now joining one another, had deepened, and the street looked more like a shallow creek than anything else.

Fifteen minutes later, he slogged back the same way. Nearing the hotel, he heard what sounded like a whistle. He stopped for a moment, listening, but the sound wasn't repeated. Back in the hotel, the clerk was no longer behind his desk. Slocum banged the bell, then took a cigarette from a small box on the desk. He lit it with a flimsy, wax-covered match and took a couple of drags before rapping the bell again, this time harder.

The sound of the bell seemed to be swallowed up by the rug and the thick draperies, dying away without an echo. With a shrug, Slocum stepped behind the desk and found his key in the appropriate cubbyhole. Taking the stairs slowly, he shook himself like a damp puppy, trying to get the worst of the rain out of his soaking clothes. His feet squished in his boots with every step, and he thought the sound must be loud enough to wake everyone in the hotel.

At the top of the stairs he moved down the long corridor, in the light thrown by a single lamp, its wick turned down so far it barely stayed lit. He found his room and slipped the key into the lock and turned the knob. The door swung open with a creak of its hinges, sounding even louder than his footsteps in the dimly lit hallway.

Closing the door, he sagged against it, every bone aching, every joint stiff from the chilling downpour. He reached into his pocket for a match, found the waterproof box trapped in the damp cloth of his pocket. He had to strike it three times before he got a spark. On the next a sputter, then a feeble glow as the flame tried to hang on.

In the dull orange light, he caught the glimmer of a lamp on a bedside table. He sat down on the bed and lifted the chimney carefully, making sure not to lose the reluctant flame. He cranked the wick up a quarter inch and brought the match to the braided cotton. The pungent scent of coal oil chewed at his nostrils, and a small tadpole of black ash wiggled up and away from the lamp's first flicker.

When the room finally filled with light, he lay back on the bed, not bothering to pull off his boots. He inhaled deeply, holding his breath and hoping that the rest of the night, at least, went more smoothly than the day. He tugged his fixings bag free of his pocket and rolled a cigarette of his own. He knew the bed was getting clammy under him, but he was too tired to care.

Removing the chimney again, he rolled toward the lamp, poked the cigarette into the flame, and when it caught let the glass clatter back into place. The first drag, after the wan taste of the hotel cigarette, soaked into him, and he held the smoke a long time, finally letting it go in a thin stream that sounded more like exasperation than a man enjoying a good smoke.

He finished the cigarette and stubbed it out in an ashtray. He closed his eyes, debating whether or not to get undressed. He fell asleep without meaning to.

When he woke up, it was dark. The lamp had burned out, and his eyes were almost useless in the gloom. Still exhausted, he wondered what had woken him. The hotel was quiet, but something must have reached him, even in his sleep. He threw his legs over the edge of the bed and let their weight carry him upright. He rubbed his eyes, trying to force them to see in the darkness. Bright flashes darted behind his fingertips.

Then he heard a thump. It was soft, as if something cushioned, as if something soft had fallen on the thick hall carpet. He strained his ears, leaning toward the door. Getting to his feet, he moved closer. He heard nothing.

At the door, he put his hand on the knob. The latch was still undone, and he reached for it. The knob began to move under his fingers. He felt it turn, then stop. A hiss on the other side of the door sounded as if someone were signaling. He backed away from the door, his hand groping along his hip for the gun that wasn't there.

He remembered he'd taken the gunbelt off, and backed toward the bed, feeling for it with one hand extended behind him. He felt the spread, then a damp spot where his muddy boots had hung over the edge of the mattress. Moving more quickly now, he swept the hand across the bed. It brushed the leather, and the cold metal of several cartridges. He snatched at it, missed, and snatched again as he heard the knob rattle softly.

Slocum snagged the gunbelt and jerked it off the bed. He heard the thump of the gun landing on the floor as the door flew open. He charged toward the door, and the dim outline of a man crouching there. A second, upright figure was already in the room, charging toward him. Slocum dove as the charging man swung something. He couldn't see it clearly, and when it caught him on the forehead, he fell to the floor.

He tried to get up, but a boot landed hard on his rib cage, knocking the wind out of him. He tried to crawl, but didn't know which way to go. The crouching figure in the doorway sprang forward. Slocum rolled, but his legs slammed into the foot of the bed, blocking him and pinning him in place.

Rough hands hauled him to his feet and something cracked against the back of his head. He felt himself falling, sagging toward the floor, until someone caught him. He felt like a bug in a spiderweb dangling there, unable to move, no matter how he twisted or turned. And like that bug, he didn't know where the spider was, just that it was coming for him.

Suddenly, the hand holding him let go, and he pitched forward onto the floor, smacking his head on a leg of the bed. He curled into a ball, wrapping his arms around his head. His back was exposed, and someone kicked him once, then again, harder. He uncoiled like an angry snake, but another foot caught him in the chest. Again the wind went out of him, and he gasped for air.

He couldn't see anyone clearly in the faint light from the doorway, and he didn't want to leave his eyes unprotected. Another boot caught him in the ribs and then in the side of

the head. He felt himself spinning out of control. Consciousness slipped away, and he reached for it the way a drowning
man grabs at a rope.

For a moment he saw everything clearly, then he felt
hands grab him by the legs. He was being dragged, and
he clawed at the carpet but couldn't slow it down. It grew
brighter, and he realized he had been dragged into the hall.
Then something slammed into his head again and the light
faded. Everything went gray, swirling like mist. His head
was spinning, and he thought he was going to throw up.

He tried to move his arms, to find something to hold on
to, and the gray thickened. He flailed his arms helplessly,
as if he were trying to fly. It was like falling off a cliff into
a deep fog.

Then he hit bottom, and everything went black.

5

The sun woke him. It was beating down on his cheek like a white-hot hammer. He groaned and rolled over. Pain shot through him like a needle driven into his shoulder. Slocum tried to move his arm, but it hurt too much. The ground was still wet, and his clothes were soaked.

Trying to sit up, he realized he was somewhere behind the hotel. Mud streaked his shirt and a gritty sand flaked off his skin as he brushed a tender spot on his jaw. Knowing where he was didn't tell him how he came to be there. He had only a dim recollection of lying down in his room. He remembered a thump in the hallway outside and getting up to see what the commotion was all about.

He remembered the door flying open, and . . . what? He couldn't remember, and his head hurt too much to try.

Hoisting himself up against a pile of old lumber, he leaned back against the boards, ignoring the stab of their corners into his back and shoulders.

Every breath hurt, and he wondered if he'd broken a rib, or if someone had broken it for him. He lay there for a long time, feeling the sun hammer away at him, feeling his mud-caked clothes stiffen in the heat. His dungarees felt as if they had been dipped in cement. Heavy and inflexible, they pressed down on his skin, scraping against him with every involuntary movement.

One arm dangled at his side, useless for the moment. He wriggled up along the stacked lumber, awkward as an inexperienced snake. When his feet were under him, he lay still, panting, trying to draw only shallow breaths to keep the stab in his side to a minimum.

He could see quite a way along the rear of the buildings, and spotted a pyramid of empty barrels that must belong to Pete Harney. He could pick out the hardware store and, in the other direction, the livery stable. The rest were just nameless shops, all built from the same bleached timbers, black water stains alternating with the dead gray of weathered wood.

Somewhere up the street a latch rattled, and Slocum tried to stand. A door banged open just beyond the barrels, and Pete Harney's familiar bulk wrestled another keg out the door. Slocum called to the bartender, but his voice was a dry rasp in his throat, more like a croak than human speech.

He called again, this time sliding along the lumber to get a little closer. Harney must have heard something, because he stopped and cocked his head for a moment. Slocum croaked again, and Harney turned. It took the bartender a moment to recognize him. Finally, Harney rushed over, wiping his hands on his apron.

"Jesus, man, what happened to you?"

Slocum allowed himself to collapse on the lumber. He shook his head. "I'm not sure."

"Who did this to you?"

"I wish to hell I knew."

"Brett Mackay, I'll bet my bottom dollar."

"I thought of that, but I just don't know."

"Man's poison. A few drinks, and . . . " Harney shrugged. "But this is different. Usually, he forgets all about it soon as you shove another beer under his nose."

"I'm not sure that's who it was, Pete."

"I am. Nobody else had a reason. Not that he did, but . . . you know what I mean. Let me help you."

He slipped Slocum's good arm over one broad shoulder and grabbed him around the waist. Taking most of the weight, he tiptoed toward the back door of the saloon.

"You okay?"

Slocum grunted. "I've been better."

"I'll bet."

Harney lugged him inside and set him gently into an overstuffed chair in the back room. Slocum sighed and allowed himself to relax, avoiding the rusty spring poking from one arm of the chair.

"You wait here. I'll go fetch Doc Chambliss."

"No, no, I'm alright."

"No argument. You just wait right here. Don't do anything stupid." Harney stripped off the damp apron and disappeared into the front of the saloon. Slocum lay back and closed his eyes. He heard Harney go out the front door, then boots on the boardwalk.

The next thing he knew, a fierce pain shot through his left arm, and he jerked his head up, nearly slamming his skull into the bifocaled eyes of a pink-cheeked man with a salt-and-pepper mustache.

Harney hovered over the man's shoulder. "He gonna be alright, Doc?"

"Christ sakes, Pete. I just got here. Let me examine the man before you ask my opinion."

Harney apologized, then said, "I think he might have a couple of busted ribs."

Chambliss sighed in exasperation. "Then what did you drag me down here for? If you know so much about medicine, why didn't you handle it yourself?"

"Sorry."

"Pete, just sit down and shut up."

"Sorry."

"Unh huh!"

The doctor opened Slocum's shirt. "I'm afraid I'm going to have to ask you to sit up. Can you do that?"

Slocum nodded, gritting his teeth and easing forward in the overstuffed chair.

"Good. Now, can you get that shirt off?"

Slocum winced as he twisted his injured left arm and tugged at the damp, matted cloth. Chambliss grabbed it by the collar and held it while Slocum pulled his arm free. Every sudden movement felt like a splash of molten lead, but he finally had the left arm clear. The right was easy.

"Jesus," Harney said, inhaling sharply. "Look at those bruises."

Slocum glanced at his chest and stomach. Palm-sized smears of dark blue and purple seemed to bleed all over his skin. He shook his head, then looked away.

"This might hurt a little," Chambliss said. His thick fingers probed each bruise in turn, and Slocum groaned. When the doctor was finished, he said, "I think you're a mighty lucky young man. Nothing broken, no ribs. Now, let me take a look at that arm."

That examination, too, was negative. Nothing but a mass of bruises. But Slocum didn't need an expert opinion to tell him that. Chambliss turned his attention to an ugly welt, just below the hairline on his right temple. "Huh! Don't even need stitches for that," he laughed.

"Doc likes to sew," Harney said. "Sometimes I think he should have been a tailor."

"Sewed you up more than once, and nobody can even tell," Chambliss snorted. "Not that anybody'd notice one more wrinkle on your old hide."

"Tough as nails, I am," Harney laughed. He seemed more relaxed, now that it was apparent Slocum wasn't seriously injured. "What now, Doc?"

"Well, I'll have to tape Mr. Slocum up, and it's going to take more tape than I got. Why don't you run down to Sam and see can you get a couple of rolls of gauze and some cloth tape."

"Anything else?"

"Not right now, Pete."

"No thimble, nothing like that?"

"Get out of here before I sew your mouth shut, you old rascal."

"Thanks, Doc," Slocum grunted.

"Don't thank me. Thank Pete. But you're going to have to take it more than a little easy for three or four days. Those are some nasty bumps and bruises. Can you do that?"

"Guess I don't have any choice."

"Not if you want to recover quickly. Got a place to stay?"

"A room at the Dry Spring Hotel."

"Unh huh. You mind if I ask you a question? I didn't want to ask in front of Pete, because he's the next best thing to a newspaper."

"Shoot."

"What did happen?"

"Don't know. I swear, I remember I was in my room, the door flew open, and that's all I can remember."

"Pete said he thought Brett Mackay had something to do with it."

"I guess he might have. We had a little run-in at Pete's. Nothing serious, but from what Pete tells me, Mackay's a bad drunk. Maybe he carried a grudge this time."

"Maybe so. It's not like him, but there's a first time for everything, I guess. You better stay out of his way, though. At least until you can move that left arm."

"Thanks, you don't have to tell me that twice."

"You get back to the hotel alright?"

"I'll manage. At least my legs work."

Harney reappeared, panting, and shoved the supplies at Chambliss. "Now, see can you bind him up without strangling the poor devil, will you, Doc?"

"Better that than choking on the miserable swill you call whiskey, Mr. Harney."

"Hell, I have three, four guys a week tell me they'd rather drink themselves to death than let you anywheres near 'em. But I'm lookin' out for Mr. Slocum here, and the last thing you need is a witness to one of your crimes."

"Pete, I have a scalpel in my bag. You open your mouth one more time, and I swear I'll take it out and use it on you."

Slocum shook his head. "You guys are gonna make me laugh, and I can't afford the pain right now."

"See that," Chambliss said, "the man was beat half silly and has more sense than you do, Pete."

Without another word, Chambliss bound Slocum's ribs and the top half of his left arm. Looking around, he spotted a spare apron, tore a rough rectangle out of it, and fashioned a sling. "You'd best keep that arm still a couple of days."

"Don't worry about that," Slocum laughed. He thought the doctor wanted to say something else, but the old man just ran a hand through his thinning hair and closed his bag.

"Pete, you gonna make yourself useful and get Mr. Slocum back to his hotel?" Chambliss seemed edgy, and he was taking it out on Pete.

"How much do I owe you, Doc?" Slocum asked.

"Let's not worry about that now. Come by the office in a couple of days, and we'll settle it up then. I want to take another look, after some of the swelling goes down. Now, how's the pain?"

Slocum swallowed hard.

"I reckon you felt better yesterday, didn't you?"

Slocum nodded.

"Look, you need rest more than you need anything. Nothing's broken, I'm pretty sure of that. And as near as

I can tell, there's no internal bleeding. But it might take a couple of days to be certain about that."

"What are you saying, Doc?" Harney asked. "You saying he's not out of the woods yet?"

"Oh, hell, Pete. Nobody's ever out of the woods. You know that. Not until they lower that pine box in the ground and cover it over. And even then, you got to get through that business with the worms. Then you're home free."

"So what *are* you saying, Doc?" Slocum tried to sit up.

"What I'm saying is that you are in for a world of pain for the next day or so. It ain't serious, I don't think, but it's gonna hurt like hell. You seen me. I checked everything. Everything's where it's supposed to be. Nothing's broken. What I want to know, you ever had laudanum?"

Slocum nodded. "Yeah, during the war."

"It works, don't it?"

"Yeah, it works. I don't like it. But I'd take it again, if I had to."

"You'll have to. You won't get any sleep otherwise. You'll twist or turn, put some pressure on something, and you'll wake right up. It'll hurt that much."

"Okay . . ."

Chambliss reopened his bag. He fished in the dark for a few moments, then brought out a small dropper-topped bottle. "Here. You take a few drops, no more'n five or six, in a half glass of water when you need to. Take less if you can. It'll keep the pain under control."

"Thanks, Doc."

Chambliss nodded. "Make sure you come see me, understand?"

Slocum watched him go. He tried to move, but the pain stabbed at him like a hot knife. His fingers closed over the small blue bottle.

"Get me a glass of water, will you, Pete?"

6

Slocum lay on the bed staring at the ceiling. The splintered door just barely hung on its hinges. It looked as if a strong gust of wind might blow it down. He didn't want to look at the door. It reminded him too much of his own life. It seemed as if he could never get a break. Whenever he thought he had things under control, something came along to explode his balloon. He was used to it by now. Maybe, he thought, even too used to it. A man ought to be in charge of his life, not its willing victim. But that was a lot easier to say than to practice.

The pain in his ribs was terrible. Doc Chambliss seemed concerned about the laudanum he had given him. But he had taken the first dose and it had worn off already. It was time for another. Slocum rolled his head toward the side table, holding his breath against the stabbing pain of even so simple a movement. In the pale light from the oil lamp, the glass seemed full of amber, like flat, watery beer. He'd used the drug before, and didn't like what it did to him. On the other hand, he didn't like what had been done to him, either, and if laudanum would kill the pain, he was not going to pass it up.

Propping himself on one elbow, he reached for the tumbler, wincing as he had to extend his fingers that one last inch. With the glass firmly in hand, he sighed, then raised it to his lips. He couldn't taste the laudanum, wondered whether the doctor had even put any in the bottle. But he drank it all, then closed his eyes and lay back.

Beside his head, just off the edge of the pillow, he could smell the gun oil. The Colt was there partly as a means of reassurance and partly because it was all that would stand between him and annihilation if Brett Mackay, or whoever had beaten him, took it into his head to come back.

Absently, he reached out and patted the sweat-darkened leather of his holster. He curled his fingers around the grip of the Colt Navy and pulled it closer, like a kid hugging a favorite toy for comfort. The lamp was running out of oil, and it began to sputter. He looked up at the wall and saw the wick coiled in the empty bowl, little pollywogs of black coiling up and away from its other end, darkening the chimney. The sputtering stopped, and the light suddenly seeped away, as if soaked up by a sponge.

He closed his eyes again, just as the lamp died altogether. The darkness wrapped around him like a second skin, and he felt safe for the first time. He knew he wasn't, he was just too damn tired to care anymore. His fingers still resting on the gun butt, he fell asleep.

He didn't sleep well, tossing and turning. Sometimes he felt as if he were suffocating, others as if he were drowning. When he finally gave up, the room was pitch black. Even the dim gray outline of the window behind its thick drapes had vanished. He wondered what time it was, and fished his pocket watch out then fumbled for a match. When he got it lit, he managed to focus his eyes just enough to read the dial. It was nearly nine o'clock. Dulled by the laudanum, he didn't realize the flame had burned too close to his fingers until, of their own accord, they let go of the match. He saw it lying on the quilt and wiped at it casually. There was none of that panic one usually feels when a flame starts to chew at clothing or a blanket. But he snuffed the flame and watched the small red circle turn from orange to red, and then wink out. Just to be sure, he poked a fingertip into the hole, then squeezed the quilt to smother any lingering ember inside it.

He heard the knock on the door only dully, as if someone were knocking on some other door in another town. Twice it came, the second time a little louder than the first. The third would have been the last, but the battered door wasn't up to resistance. The latch broke free, and the door swung inward. The doorway was transformed into a pale orange block. Slocum fumbled for the Colt, even while his eyes tried to adjust to the sudden apparition.

As he tugged the revolver free of its holster, he already had begun to realize it couldn't be Brett Mackay come to pay his respects. The silhouette was far too small. Other than that, he was able to discern almost nothing. Rather than enter uninvited, the figure rapped on the doorframe with small knuckles.

"Hello . . . ?"

The hushed whisper sounded almost like a snake's hissing. "Anybody there? Mr. Slocum?"

"Come in," he said, startled at the sound of his own voice. It sounded louder than he'd meant it to, and strange. He was hoarse, and the words croaked out of him.

But as loud as it had seemed to him, the invitation had not been heard. "Mr. Slocum, are you in there?"

He croaked again, and this time she heard him. He knew it was a woman because she had stopped whispering.

The shadowy figure stepped through the doorway. "Can you turn on the light?"

"No. Can't get up," he said.

"Where is it?"

"Out of oil."

"Wait a minute. . . . " She turned and walked out into the hall. Even in the better light he couldn't make out her features. In a fraction of a second she was gone. He lay there, starting to wonder whether he had imagined the whole thing, when the hall light grew brighter. A moment later she was back in the doorway, splashing a giant shadow on the wall behind her. Even with the lamp cradled beneath her chin, he didn't recognize her. His eyes were blurry and unfocused. His tongue felt as if it were coated with wool. It was worse than a hangover, and he wondered why until he remembered the laudanum.

The woman stepped into the room, glancing at the shattered door with what could have been either curiosity or amusement. He was in no shape to decide and he didn't try.

She thrust the lamp out before her and circled the bed, looking for something. When she found the lamp on the wall, she set hers down and reached up for the empty, carefully lifting it from its sconce.

She dropped out of sight for a moment, and he heard a small door latch click. A moment later and she reappeared. She refilled the reservoir of the wall lamp, adjusted the wick, and pulled a match from her shirt pocket. Relighting the wall lamp, she turned the wick up a bit, replaced the chimney, and returned the lamp to the wall bracket. Leaving the borrowed lamp on the table, she walked to the foot of the bed. She seemed to study him for a long moment, a certain curiosity coloring her detachment.

"You don't remember me, do you?"

"I'm not sure. I can't see straight at the moment."

She noticed the Colt in his hand and pointed at it. "Were you going to shoot me?"

"Depends," he said, trying to smile. His lips wouldn't work, and he felt as if his face had started to melt.

"On what?"

"On whether or not you were you or somebody else."

"I take it being me is alright."

"What?"

"You haven't shot me . . . yet."

"That's right." His words sounded odd to him, slurred, as if he were drunk. For a moment he wondered why, then again remembered the drug.

"Are you drunk or something?"

He shook his head, not trusting himself with words.

She leaned over the foot of the bed to scrutinize him. "You don't look too good. Shall I fetch a doctor?"

Slocum gestured toward the small bottle on the table. "Already had me a doctor. That's why I sound like this."

She moved around the corner of the bed and walked to the small night table. Snatching the bottle, she moved closer to the lamps and read the label. "No wonder. . . . " She turned to look at him over her shoulder. The rest of her body followed slowly, but she never took her eyes off him. "You're not . . . "

He shook his head. "No, ma'am. I'm not addicted, if that's what you want to know. But I feel a whole lot better right now with it than without it."

She moved closer again. "I heard what happened. I think I owe you an apology."

"Why? You sic Mackay on me?"

"Who's Mackay?"

"Brett Mackay, the fellow I figure must have used me for his own personal war drum."

"No. I don't know who that is. I just meant . . . well, I jumped to conclusions last night. I thought you had attacked my father. Now I know you didn't, and I guess your sticking up for him is what brought this on."

"Probably not. Mackay was spoiling for a fight. If it hadn't been your father, it would have been something else set him off. And if it hadn't been me, somebody else would have had his ribs stove in. Your father was just an excuse and I was just handy. And stupid."

"How so?"

"I knew what he was like. I should have been more careful."

Slocum found talking too much of an effort, and he let his words trail off.

"I suppose I should introduce myself. I'm Cordelia Ramsey." She stretched out a hand, and he grasped it limply, holding it just long enough to wonder at the strength of so small a hand.

"Unusual name," he croaked.

"My father's idea, of course. My sisters and I are all named after Shakespearean heroines. Portia and Juliet—those are my sisters—think it's silly, but I kind of like it."

"I do too."

"I came to apologize, as I said. But I see now I should do more."

"No need."

"Nonsense. You can't stay here. How will you eat? You can't take care of yourself."

"Just need to rest up for a day or two, then I'll be able to get around. And right now, I don't feel like eating. Don't think I could even hold anything down."

"Are you certain?"

Slocum nodded.

"Well, if you change your mind . . . "

"I won't."

"I'll look in on you in the morning, just in case."

"That's alright."

"What about that door? Aren't you afraid, being so vulnerable?"

"The door was okay before this happened. It didn't help then, and I don't guess it would be any more useful now."

"Still . . . "

"Besides, you can't stay here, and I can't run away."

"Something tells me you wouldn't run away even if you were able to."

"Do I look that stupid?"

Slocum tried to grin, but the attempt misfired. And Cordelia answered the question straight. "I didn't mean that. I meant you didn't seem like the kind of man who would allow himself to be bullied."

"You know a lot about that kind of man, do you?"

"Not from life, no. I've never met such a man. But Shakespeare wrote about them. They must exist."

Slocum shook his head. "For poets and dreamers, maybe, ma'am. But—"

"Never mind." She started toward the door suddenly, and he thought he might have offended her. But she turned, and said, "I'll be back in a few minutes."

Slocum stared at the block of light where her shadow had seemed to vaporize. He was aware only of his pain, and the rasp of breath in his throat. His eyes blinked and for a while he counted them but soon lost track in the laudanum haze.

When she reappeared, it was as if she had never been gone. "Don't let him out of your sight, Louis," she said. Slocum was puzzled. He saw no one but Cordelia in the doorway.

"I won't," someone answered, the voice frail and high-pitched. Slocum shook his head and tried to screw his eyes into focus. He blinked, and in the brief, blurry interlude something, or someone, had materialized at Cordelia's side.

"And don't let him get out of bed. Not for any reason."

The small figure, who had to be Louis, shook its strange head. "You bet, Cory."

She turned to Slocum. "This is a friend of mine, Louis Marillac, Mr. Slocum. He'll keep an eye on you. I'll be back in the morning." Without another word, she was gone.

Louis walked toward the bed. As he drew closer, it looked as if his head were floating all by itself, just above the bedcovers. Then he moved alongside, and Slocum slid over a few inches. Louis stopped right beside the night table. His eyes were at the same level as Slocum's own.

He smiled, displaying a double row of uneven teeth, each one filed to a glittering point.

"No jokes," he said. Then brought his hand up and placed a pearl-handled Colt .45 on the bed. "It's not a toy, Mr. Slocum. I assure you."

Slocum shook his head again. When he realized Louis was still there, he closed his eyes. Nothing else made sense.

7

Slocum slept for three hours. The laudanum started to wear off, and the pain in his ribs woke him. The light was turned down to little more than a dim glow. He groaned, and a small shadow at the foot of the bed suddenly darted toward him. Groggily, he groped for the pistol, but it was no longer beside the pillow.

The light grew brighter as he tried to sit up. He saw Louis then, only vaguely aware that he had seen the little man before.

"Looking for this?" Louis asked, holding the Colt Navy by the barrel.

"I guess I was." Slocum fell back on the pillow, turning his head toward the lamp. Louis waddled toward him on his tiny legs, and Slocum almost smiled, in spite of the pain.

"You think I can't use a gun?" Louis asked.

"No, why?"

"You're smiling at something. The shape you're in, it must be pretty funny."

He realized the little man must have been offended.

"I didn't mean anything," Slocum assured him.

"Sure you did. But I'm used to it. You can't be this short all your life and not get used to it. If I let what other people thought get to me, I'd never leave the house."

"I guess you're right."

"I *am* right." Louis approached the bed. "You should go back to sleep."

"Can't." Slocum reached for the small bottle of laudanum. His hand trembled with the exertion. Rolling on his side, he just barely grabbed the pitcher of water, but when he tried to fill the glass, it spilled all over.

"Let me do it." Louis snatched the pitcher away and stood on tiptoe to pour a tumbler full of water. Setting the pitcher back down, he took the laudanum bottle from Slocum's slack fingers. "This is bad stuff," he said. "Don't get used to it."

"You sound as if you know all about it."

Louis didn't answer. He opened the bottle. "How many drops?"

"Six, I think."

"Not too bad. That won't hurt you." He decanted a half-dozen drops, letting each one swell until its own weight tore it free of the dropper. The water grew slightly darker, and Louis mixed the medicine with a glass rod before handing the tumbler to Slocum.

He watched quietly as Slocum drained the glass in one swallow. Taking the empty glass, he set it on the table, then walked back to his chair at the foot of the bed.

As Slocum closed his eyes, just the top of Louis's head was visible. He opened them again, trying to impose his will on a room that seemed bent on disappearing. The room started to shimmer, as if it were dissolving, and he felt the first stirrings of nausea. He opened his eyes wider, but everything had started to spin, and he felt as if the bed were lifting off the floor. The ceiling dissolved, and he closed his eyes again.

He could hear, but he was afraid to open his eyes, afraid he would vomit, maybe even choke. He could hear, but there was nothing but a sibilant whistle as Louis ran through a smattering of tunes in short phrases, most of which were unfamiliar. The sound was pleasant enough, and he relaxed a little, slowly letting the tension drain out of him. He stopped fighting the laudanum, and let the spin carry him away.

Once he thought he heard Cordelia, and he opened his eyes, but Louis still sat, quietly now, at the foot of the bed. The light had been turned down again, and if Cordelia was there, he couldn't see her. Too sleepy to do anything more than roll his head from side to side, he tried to listen, but heard nothing.

Finally, he lost consciousness altogether. As the last glimmer of awareness began to fade, he imagined himself in an open boat, maybe a canoe, drifting downstream and out into the ocean. He had only seen the ocean once, and it seemed then like the greatest mystery in the world. It seemed only fitting that he slide into it now, and a kind of half smile curled his lips. He felt the movement of muscles in his face and tried to nod his approval, but it was beyond him.

The pain was gone, and he found it hard to remember what it felt like. When that, too, proved too much for him, he faded out completely.

A rap on the door tugged at his senses, trying to pull him back. He saw a block of light surround the top of Louis's head, like an oblong halo, then someone entered the room. Just a shadow, it was impossible to recognize who it might be. He thought again of Cordelia, but the shadow seemed too large for her. He wondered whether he was measuring her against Louis, then lost control again, drifting like a kid's paper boat on a rain-swollen creek.

The shadow came toward him, standing beside the bed. He saw Louis turn, but the little man said nothing, and the figure beside him stayed silent. He faded out again, this time too far gone to fight the drug.

In the morning, Slocum felt much better. Louis watched while he swung his legs over the side of the bed. He felt a little dizzy, but with effort he could stop the room from spinning. He got shakily to his feet, almost losing his balance for a few seconds. He felt himself swaying, and there was nothing he could do about it, but the sensation passed as Louis watched him in silence.

A couple of steps restored his confidence, and he let go of the bed completely. His upper body was still wracked with pain, and it hurt to move too quickly. The injured arm gave him the most trouble. It hurt too much to hold it still, and letting it dangle at his side hurt even more. He remembered the sling, and turned back to the bed. He spotted it on the table, and took a half-dozen tiny steps, reached for it with the good arm, and slipped it over his head.

Getting the arm into the cloth was not quite so easy. Every flex sent a surge of pain through the biceps, and he gritted his teeth to keep from complaining.

Louis finally spoke. "You're going to need help for a couple of days yet."

"Maybe not."

The little man twisted his lips into a scornful smile. "All you big guys are the same. You're all too tough for your own good. You think wanting to do something makes you able. It's like you think pain is beneath your dignity."

"What do you know about it?" Slocum snapped.

"Pain? I know more about pain than you'll ever know."

"From what, bumping your head on tables?"

"I knew you wouldn't be able to resist that."

"What?"

"Commenting on my size. You see a dwarf, you immediately feel superior. *Dwarf*, like we were some kind of pet animal or something."

"I didn't mean it like that."

"How did you mean it? How else could you have meant it?"

Slocum started to answer when a heavy fist rapped on the broken door. Slocum looked immediately for his gun, then remembered Louis had it.

"Come in," Slocum said.

The door swung open, and he was relieved to see Pete Harney, still wearing a damp apron, his thick hands closed over his gut.

"Morning, John," Harney said.

Slocum shook his head. "Pete . . . "

"You alright?"

"Sure, why wouldn't I be?"

"Mackay was making a lot of noise last night. I thought he might have paid you a visit."

"I have a bodyguard." Slocum indicated Louis.

The bartender grinned. "Guess I was worried for nothing, huh?"

Louis spun the cylinder in Slocum's revolver. He looked at Harney without saying a word. Harney scowled, letting his eyebrows collapse in toward his nose and eyes. "Watch what you're doing with that thing, Shorty," he snapped.

"Don't worry about a thing, Tubby. I know what I'm doing."

Harney frowned noticeably. "Watch your mouth, shrimp."

"Alright, you two," Slocum said. "You're supposed to be on the same side, aren't you?"

"Yeah, sure, John. I just . . . I mean, he doesn't have to get insulting."

"What about Mackay, Pete? He mention me by name?"

Harney shook his head. "Didn't mention any names, but it's pretty clear he was talking about you."

"What did he say, then? Exactly . . . "

"Said some people don't know when to quit. Said some people have to learn things the hard way."

"That's just booze talking. Mackay's a bigmouth, but I don't think he's much of a threat."

"Maybe not, but I'd be careful, I was you. You ought to go someplace till you mend up a little."

"Where the hell could I go?"

"Hell, I don't know." He turned to glance at the door. "But this place sure ain't safe. Even with a watchdog like him." He jerked a thumb toward Louis, who seemed uncertain whether Harney had meant to insult him again, this time indirectly.

"No need to find a place to stay," Louis put in. "That's already been taken care of."

"That's news to me," Slocum said.

"Miss Cordelia wants you to stay with the troupe. That way there'll always be someone around. Arrangements have already been made."

"First I've heard of it," Slocum said.

"We worked it out last night, while you were sleeping."

"So, she *was* here then. I didn't imagine it."

Louis nodded. "She'll be here in a little while. She had to make some adjustments first."

"Suppose I don't want to go, Louis."

"You don't have anything to say about it. Not really. Miss Cordelia always gets what she wants. Besides, you'd be a fool not to accept her offer."

"The little guy makes sense, John," Harney volunteered.

Cordelia appeared in the doorway before Slocum could disagree.

"Ready to move, Mr. Slocum?"

"Move where?"

"I think you'd better spend a couple of days with us. We can look after you better if you're with the troupe."

"I can look after myself."

"No, you can't."

She stepped up to him and placed both hands on his

chest. He winced at the pressure, and when she pushed him, he nearly lost his balance. Harney grabbed Slocum to keep him from falling to the floor.

"You see?" Cordelia asked. "You can't look after yourself at all, can you?"

Slocum didn't answer.

"Say it! Say, 'I can't look after myself.' "

Slocum refused, and Cordelia laughed. "You're such a fraud, Mr. Slocum. You truly are, did you know that?"

When he still refused to answer, she turned to Harney. "Can you give us a hand getting our Hercules down to the wagon?"

"Sure thing, miss." Harney looked at Slocum for a minute. "She's right, John," he said. "It's the best thing. It really is."

Slocum knew he was beaten. He leaned on the big bartender, and let Harney half carry him toward the door. Cordelia gathered up his few things, then stepped into the hall, just ahead of the two men.

"Louis, you go on down and get in the wagon. This might take a few minutes." The little man nodded. He still carried Slocum's Colt, and draped the gunbelt over his shoulder before squeezing between Harney and the doorframe.

Slocum, still groggy, blinked away the brighter light of the hallway. He was only too conscious of how easily Pete Harney was handling him. They were right and he knew it, but he couldn't bring himself to admit it. He would be no match at all for Brett Mackay. Not for a few days, at least.

As they slowly descended the stairs, Slocum nearly lost his footing, suddenly throwing his full weight onto Harney. The barman tugged him back, wrenching Slocum's ribs and sending a wave of fire through his midsection.

At the front door, Slocum saw a wagon, its tailgate down. Louis sat on the front seat, Slocum's pistol prominently displayed. Ten feet away, Brett Mackay leaned against the hotel window.

"Going somewhere, Slocum?" He laughed. "Can't say I blame you, cowboy. But you know something? You got to run a long time to get away from me."

Louis bristled, and twirled the cylinder of the big Navy revolver.

Mackay laughed again. "Ain't no midget gonna make a difference, neither."

Slocum bit his lip and watched the big cowboy sidle away. He didn't like feeling helpless. But for the first time since the beating, he realized that's exactly what he was: helpless.

8

Slocum lay in the wagon bed, trying desperately to stop himself from rolling into either side wall. On his back, he was forced to look straight up into the sun. He clamped his lids shut, and the sun turned them a brilliant red. It felt as if they were about to catch fire and burn away, leaving his eyes to the mercy of the sun.

He could hear Louis and Cordelia talking, but with the creaking of the wheels and the steady clomp of the horses' hooves, he couldn't make out what they were saying. The two blocks seemed to take forever, and when the wagon finally lurched around the last corner, he was astonished to see a huge striped tent slide by on the right-hand side.

He wanted to ask where he was being taken, but was unable to get their attention. The wagon jolted to a halt after making a wide half circle around the red and white canvas tent. Louis turned to grin at him, tilting his head, Slocum thought purposefully, so that the sun glinted off his filed teeth.

"How do you feel, Mr. Slocum?"

"Where the hell are we?"

Louis swept his arm vaguely in the direction of the tent. "The theatuh, my good man."

Cordelia scowled at him, and Louis looked apologetic. "It's Professor Ramsey's traveling theater." Louis glanced at Cordelia to see whether his second explanation was less offensive. Apparently it was.

"Just wait here a moment, Mr. Slocum." Cordelia jumped down from the wagon seat, and he heard her boots crunch on the dry, sandy soil. Louis swung his legs around and let his feet dangle into the wagon box.

"She loves her father," Louis said.

Slocum was caught off guard by the observation, but when he asked Louis what he meant, the little man shook his head. "You'll come to know on your own, or you'll never know."

"Why are you trying so damned hard to be mysterious, Louis?"

"Because life is a mystery, Johnny. Because I'm alive, and I am mystified. What other reason do I need?"

Slocum shook his head. "I wish to hell I knew what was going on here."

"It's quite simple, really."

"Then I wish someone would explain it to me."

"Perhaps Miss Cordelia will. If you ask her. And if she's in the right frame of mind."

"And if not?"

"What can I tell you, Johnny? Life's hard on us all."

Slocum heard boots on the sand again, this time more than two. Cordelia bobbed into view, followed by two dandified young men; neither of whom could have weighed more than a hundred and fifty pounds.

"Take it easy with him," Cordelia said, stepping aside. The two dandies grabbed him by the legs and tugged him toward the tail gate. Slocum groaned at the sudden strain on his rib cage, and tried to pull a leg free, but the delicate-looking hands that held him were surprisingly strong.

A moment later he tilted up, and his feet thudded to the ground. The shock sent a wave of nausea rolling upward, and he thought for a moment he was going to pass out. But the seizure passed, and he found himself draped across the backs of the two fancy boys, one arm over each pair of fragrant shoulders. The young men were bony, but strong. They handled him easily, letting his feet drag across the sand like the struts of a broken *travois*.

Ahead, he saw a semicircle of wagons, each covered in the same striped canvas as the tent, each sporting a folding stairway sprung from its rear. The makeshift doorways were draped in heavy, colorless cloth. There were eight altogether, and the young men headed straight for the second in line.

In no time, he found himself hauled up the rickety steps and lying on a thick, blanketed mattress suspended from one wall of the wagon, propped by folding legs on the interior edge. As a bed it was no great shakes, but it was better than lying on the floor of the wagon.

The dandies left, giggling to one another, and Cordelia drew up a chair and sat beside him. "How are you feeling?" she asked.

"This isn't necessary, Miss Ramsey."

"You're in no shape to decide that."

"Why are you doing it? What is going on?"

"You tried to help my father. I attacked you wrongly, and so I owe you twice, once for your good intentions and once for my misreading them. All I'm trying to do is to make sure that you are well enough to fend for yourself. It's our fault this happened. It doesn't seem right to walk away from that kind of responsibility."

"You're one damn exasperating Samaritan, you know that?"

"When was the last time you ate a decent meal?" She ignored his question and stared hard at him, waiting for an answer to her own.

"I forget."

"That's what I thought. I'll be back."

"Aren't you going to tell me not to go anywhere?"

"I leave the jokes to Louis."

"He's not funny either. . . . "

Cordelia stood and left the wagon. He felt it shift under her tread, then bounce as she stepped onto the ground. He lay there waiting for her to return, thinking he had never felt so helpless in his life. He didn't like the way it felt. It went against everything he believed in. A man was supposed to be able to take care of himself. If he couldn't do that, he had no right to take up space. But being trapped there in the wagon, feeling very much like some sort of circus freak kept in the dark between exhibits, he was starting to change his mind.

When Cordelia returned, he still hadn't been able to sort it all out. She sat beside him and fed him some sort of broth from a wooden spoon. It hurt to tilt his head up, but there was no other way to get the broth down without spilling it all over.

She dabbed away at his chest with a thick linen napkin, and he felt like a child. He wanted to tell her she should put a bib on him, but it was too close to the truth for him to say it aloud. The broth went down easily, and he was beginning to overcome his embarrassment at being so dependent on the charity of others.

On the same tray she had a covered dish, and when the broth was all gone she lifted the pewter lid to uncover a steaming plate of stew. She had cut the meat into tiny pieces, and the vegetables were soft enough to cut with a fork. Patiently, she shoveled the food into his mouth then waited for him to chew and swallow.

As much as it hurt to move, he knew he needed the nourishment. And the food was more than passable. "You're not a bad cook," he said between mouthfuls.

"Thanks, but I didn't make any of this. My father did."

"The professor? He can cook this well?"

"My father is a very special man, Mr. Slocum. There is no one at all like him."

"Children should feel that way about their parents."

"I suppose so. What about you? Do you feel that way about your father?"

"I suppose I did . . . when he was alive."

"I'm sorry, I didn't mean to—"

"It's alright. Yes, you're right, he *was* special. I always felt it. But I guess I didn't let him know. It's kind of hard to be . . . honest, I guess. With your father, I mean."

"Yes, it is. Even for me."

She held his head while he took a drink of water. "I'm sorry water's all there is to drink."

"Never mind. It's just right."

"Tomorrow we'll have to take a look at those ribs of yours."

"Doc said I should stop by and see him as soon as I felt up to it."

"Will you be up to it tomorrow?"

Slocum shook his head. "I don't know. Sometimes, I think I can get up whenever I want. Other times, I don't know if it'll ever stop hurting."

"The medicine helps, does it?"

He nodded his head. "Yes, it does. I don't like the way it makes me feel, my head I mean, it does funny things. But at least it kills the pain for a while."

Cordelia prepared another draft of the laudanum for him. She held it to his lips, and he gulped it down in three quick swallows. "Try to get some rest. I'll look in on you later."

"Thank you, Miss Ramsey."

She didn't answer. She started to say something, then stopped, her mouth suddenly frozen in midword. Her eyes misted over, and he noticed for the first time their striking, almost iridescent blue color.

He lay back and closed his eyes. He felt her hands tuck a blanket in around him, and the sensation seemed somehow odd. He started that unnerving drift again, his head growing light. Even with his eyes closed he felt as if the world were spinning very fast, threatening to throw him off, the way a turning wagon wheel threw mud with every rotation.

He was only dimly aware that she had left when the wagon tilted again under her weight on the steps. Alone, the canvas drawn taut across the opening, he lay there like an insect wrapped in silk, waiting for some momentous change to overtake him. It almost seemed as if, after a night in the wagon, he would be reborn. All his aches and bruises would be gone, and he'd be a brand-new man, ready to give the world another chance. He only wished it could be so abrupt and so total.

He woke several times, noting the passage of the day by the increased level of pain in his battered body and the progressively darker cast of the canvas. When he awoke for what seemed like the tenth time, it was dark. It was no longer possible to see anything through the canvas, even to get some sense of its contours. It was pitch black outside, and deathly still.

He lay there, straining his ears for a cricket, a tree frog, some sound, however slight, to prove that he was not alone in a black world. But the insects were quiet. Once, an owl started to hoot, then swallowed the sound as if something had startled it.

He heard footsteps on the crunchy gravel beside the wagon. In the pitch black canvas, he thought it must be like that for a man buried alive, listening to someone walk past his grave, unable to summon help. Another set of feet approached, lighter this time, and seemed to stop not ten feet away from the covered wagon.

"Well," a woman's voice whispered, "have you made up your mind?"

"Fifty. I already told you." The response was even more hoarse, but much deeper, obviously the voice of a man.

"But will you do it?"

"Why shouldn't I?"

"No reason."

"You got the money?"

"Of course. You don't think I'd try to swindle you, do you?"

The man laughed. "How stupid do you think I am? Of course I think you'd try to swindle me. Why shouldn't you? That's why I want to get paid first."

"You must think me the fool, then. Why should I pay you before you deliver?"

"Alright, I suppose you have a point." The man laughed again. "You're not as dumb as I thought."

"You'd do well to keep that in mind."

"Half up front. Do it, and we have a deal."

The woman didn't answer right away. Slocum tried to get closer, leaning way over the side of the bed. There was something familiar about both voices. But he couldn't quite place either of them.

"Your friend's here," the woman said.

"Who?"

"The cowboy. Slocum."

"You think that makes a difference?"

"Does it?"

"He's in no shape to be a problem. Not for me. No, it doesn't make a difference."

"Good. I was afraid he might be difficult, an unexpected wrinkle, somebody you might prefer not to have to deal with."

"Don't worry about it. You got time to take a little walk?"

"What for?" She sounded startled, and a little amused.

"Why do you think?"

"My husband wouldn't like it."

"All the more reason for you to come. Am I right?"

The woman didn't respond, but both sets of feet moved off in the same direction.

Slocum got out of the bed, crawling on his knees to the canvas flap over the rear of the wagon. He parted it carefully and looked out into a moonless night. But he couldn't see a soul. The effort took its toll on him, and he hauled himself weakly back to the bed, barely managing to crawl over the side before losing consciousness.

Even in the semidrugged sleep he could hear the voices, and wondered whose they were.

9

When dawn broke, Slocum felt better. Something about the night had convinced him he would be better off leaving. He couldn't explain it, just a feeling deep in his gut. These people might mean well, he thought, but there is no way in hell I am spending another day here. He tried to get up. It hurt like hell, but not enough to keep him prisoner another day.

He gathered his things and slipped out of the wagon, careful not to make a noise. Louis slept on a pallet on the floor. The little man was snoring loudly, but Slocum didn't want to take a chance on waking him. He didn't want to hurt anyone's feelings, especially not Cordelia's, but enough, in this case, was plenty.

His muscles loosed up a little as he walked toward the

61

center of town. Slocum retrieved his horse, but chose to walk a little more. He led the chestnut down the center of the street, then tied him off in front of the doctor's office.

Climbing the stairs to the sign that read simply DOC CHAMBLISS, he hoped the sawbones was in. It was just after dawn, but a light burned under the door, and Chambliss stomped over to open it without a moment's hesitation. It didn't take long to convince Chambliss he wasn't going to stay around. The doctor was against his leaving, but he seemed to recognize how determined his patient was. He shook Slocum's hand and watched him descend the stairs sideways. When Slocum reached the bottom Chambliss said, "You be careful, now, Slocum. And let me see you again in about a week."

Slocum nodded. "Sure thing, Doc." Then he watched Chambliss, shaking his head, turn and reenter the office. When the door closed, Slocum stepped into the street, careful not to stretch his ribs too much.

Getting into the saddle was the easy part, Slocum thought, as he draped his leg over the skittish horse. Making the ride to the Double Rocker was going to be a small version of hell. His ribs still ached, but he didn't need the sling anymore. He understood what his grandmother meant about thanking God for small favors. The irony hit him like a load of double-O buckshot.

But he was alive, and the sooner he got back to the spread and back to work, the sooner he could put the whole business behind him. And that's all he really wanted to do. He kicked the chestnut, and it shook its head before starting to move, as if to let his rider know who was really in charge.

As the town fell away behind him, Slocum looked back once, just to make sure, then pushed the big horse a little harder. The open country rose gently toward the foothills, every ridge a little higher than the last then sloping down to a valley not quite as deep as the last. Slocum was thankful for the easy terrain.

So far, so good, he thought. If he stayed stiff and straight, almost nothing hurt. He held the reins in his right hand, letting the left drape over his thigh. As long as he didn't have to move the arm quickly, it left him alone. Twenty miles was a snap for him, ordinarily. But the conditions weren't quite ordinary, and he didn't want to wear himself out.

His strength was still low. Three days in bed seemed to have soaked it out of him, the way a sponge soaked up water. A half hour seemed like a week of riding, and that meant he still had several weeks to go when he hit a stand of firs, the first benchmark on the route home. He reined in as he entered the trees, enjoying the shade. He was soaked with sweat, and the high sun seemed to be concentrating all its heat on him. He could feel it through his shirt, and the back of his neck had already begun to sting.

A small stream ran through the valley floor, and he let the chestnut amble toward it and stroked the big horse's neck while it drank. Four hours, he kept telling himself, just four hours. Harney had told him he was crazy to push himself too hard so soon, but Slocum was nothing if not stubborn. He couldn't shake the feeling that Dry Spring and Clayton Ramsey were sulfur and saltpeter. All it took was a little charcoal and a spark, and there'd be one hell of an explosion.

It wouldn't be long.

The water looked tempting, but getting off the horse would be a mistake. When the horse had satisfied its thirst, Slocum jerked the reins and urged him across the creek. He had another fifty yards of shade before the blazing sun would have him at its mercy again. But there was no point in postponing the inevitable. The longer he waited, the more exhausted he would be. The tension of sitting stock-still on a moving horse was draining what little energy he had.

Out in the open again, he glanced up at the sun, shielding his eyes with one hand. Not a single cloud offered relief, and Slocum shrugged before kicking the horse into a slow trot. Every hoofbeat seemed to rattle his joints, and his teeth cracked together. He gave it up reluctantly, letting his body move now, and it took less out of him.

But it still hurt like hell.

Far ahead, like stick figures on a distant chalkboard, he saw two riders, heading parallel to the next ridge. It was too far for him to see much more than their outlines, and even they were blurred by the brilliant sun. He squinted against the bright light, but it did no good. They were going flat out, kicking up a plume of yellow dust. He watched them for a quarter of a mile before they slanted away and down the far side out of sight.

Heading up the long, easy slope, he spotted a small herd of pronghorn, seven or eight head, and he slowed to watch them lope across the hillside. They must have been frightened by the riders he'd seen. He hadn't heard a shot, but the antelope were always skittish, and it didn't take much to set them flying.

He was near the top of the hill now, and already he was soaked through with sweat. A stand of cottonwoods near the valley floor offered some relief, and he slanted to the right, pushing the chestnut a little harder. Another creek, this one smaller, almost like an afterthought, angled through the valley floor, squiggling in its course like a frightened worm. It caught the bright sun and scattered reflected light up into the trees where it passed through the cottonwoods.

Ten minutes of pure agony brought him to the shade. He slowed the horse and let it walk the last few yards. A few scattered boulders littered the creekbank, and Slocum headed for the largest of them. Gripping the reins tightly in one fist, he held the horse steady while he shifted his weight enough to slide his leg up and over. With both feet planted securely on a boulder, he let the rock take his weight, then climbed to the ground with a sigh of relief.

He let the horse wander toward the water and leaned back against the rock, breathing as deeply as his ribs allowed.

Every breath felt as if someone were stripping the skin off his chest with a rusty knife. For a moment, he saw specks of light circling in front of his eyes, and he wondered whether it had been smart to leave Dry Spring so soon.

Ray Henderson had been to see him, and told him his job was being held and not to worry. But Slocum was not a man to let anything slide. It could become a habit, one you couldn't get rid of. If you had work, then you worked. It was that simple. And he wasn't about to let a few bruised ribs come between him and his responsibilities.

When the dancing lights receded and his vision cleared, he shook his head and walked stiffly toward the water. He dropped slowly to his knees, letting his legs do all the work. Slocum pushed his hat back off his forehead. Bracing himself with stiff arms, he leaned down for a drink. He was about to plunge his face into the cold, clear water, when he noticed something odd.

He stared at the water for a few seconds, not even sure he saw anything at all. Tilting his head from side to side, he examined it from several angles, but it always looked the same. He closed his eyes for a minute, then shook his head once more, just to make sure.

When he opened his eyes again, it was still there. The water didn't look right. It was discolored, somehow. Barely noticeable, but definite. He scooped a handful of the cold water and brought it close to examine it. But against his palm, he noticed nothing unusual. But he was sure. He dug a handkerchief out of his pocket and slid it into the creek. There, against the white of the cloth, there was no mistaking the discoloration. It was sort of rusty, a reddish brown so pale you almost had to be looking for it to see it. He wondered how he had noticed it himself, then realized a small patch of white sand in the creekbed had made it possible.

Slocum dried his hands on his dungarees and painfully cranked himself back to his feet. Stepping into the shallow water, he started upstream. He placed each foot carefully before letting it take his weight. The scattered rocks on the streambed were slippery, some of them mossy, and he couldn't afford to fall. If he landed the wrong way, he might lay here for days before anyone found him. If he didn't drown.

His horse nickered, and he turned sharply, sending a stab of pain through his chest, but the animal just watched him through expressionless eyes, staring back as if to ask what he wanted.

He hadn't gone more than thirty feet when he found it. And he was sorry he had.

He saw the hand first. Ten yards upstream, it lay, palm up, in the water, the fingers slightly curled, just above the surface. Staring at it, frozen in place, Slocum didn't want to believe it. He could see the sleeve of a shirt angling up into some tall grass. Blood soaked the bottom of the sleeve and dribbled slowly into the water. He started to move, ignoring the risk, and covered the last twenty feet at a run.

His feet still in the creek, he knelt on the rocky bank. The man lay on his face, and Slocum saw the ugly hole in his back, a bright red stain, already darkening at the edges as the blood had begun to dry. Backshot. And his mind flashed immediately to the two riders he'd seen on the ridge.

He rolled the body over, and recognized the dead man immediately. It was Randolph Moseley, one of Ramsey's troupe. One of the fancy boys. He was unarmed, as usual. Slocum doubted whether the kid even knew how to use a gun. Who in the hell would have any reason to shoot him?

He tossed his hat into the grass and placed an ear against the kid's chest, on the off chance he was wrong. But the heart was silent, the chest motionless. The kid's eyes, their blue beginning to cloud over, stared up past Slocum's head and through the cottonwoods. He didn't know whether they looked surprised, as if someone he trusted had turned on him, or if every pair of eyes was surprised by death, no matter how expected. They seemed to accuse him of guilty knowledge, and Slocum pressed the lids closed with a callused thumb.

Taking a deep breath, he considered his options. Unsure whether he could handle the body himself, he debated leaving it where it lay and riding back to Dry Spring for the sheriff. But the thought of scavengers ripping at the corpse made the decision for him. He'd seen a lot of violent death, caused some of it himself, and narrowly avoided his own on occasion. He was a hard man in a hard country. But Moseley was not. He didn't deserve to be left there for the bugs and the buzzards.

Slocum stood up, feeling for a moment as if someone were watching him. He bent to retrieve his hat and then climbed out of the creek. It was too far from town for the kid to have walked. There ought to be a horse around somewhere. He stepped into the cottonwoods, following scuff marks on the ground. It looked as if Moseley had put up a fight and been dragged down to the creek before being shot in the back.

Backtracking along the trail, he noticed two sets of boot prints, one with a squared toe, the other more pointy, in the occasional patches of bare ground among the leaf mulch. One print, looking as if it had been placed by an artist, had been crushed deeply into some moss. It was perfect, even to a nick in the heel. The left foot of a big man. Slocum wondered whether it would be of any use, then shook off the thought. In hard country, a man caught with a smoking gun still in his hand got off more often than not. There was no chance of catching and punishing the killers, unless there had been an eyewitness, someone who not only saw what happened, but who would be willing to stand up in court and testify.

Fat chance, Slocum thought.

He heard a rustling among the underbrush and spun toward the sound, reaching for his Colt at the same instant. Something thumped on the ground, and Slocum edged toward the brush, ducking a little to cut down on his target. He waved the Colt from side to side.

"Anybody there?"

His voice died in the leaves. Behind him he could hear the sound of the creek burbling over stones. And over a dead man's hand.

He poked the Colt into the leaves, then parted the brush with his left arm. Slipping in among the branches, ignoring the way they tugged at his clothes and jabbed his tender ribs, he cocked the revolver and called again. "Hello . . . ?"

Again, he got no answer. Breaking through the clump of undergrowth, he sighed. A horse, its reins trailing on the ground, nipped at some grass, occasionally shuffling its feet. The animal eyed him curiously, backing away a couple of feet. Slocum holstered the Colt and moved slowly toward the animal, one hand extended for the reins. He didn't recognize the horse, but it had to belong to Moseley. And even if it didn't, it solved the problem.

Snatching the reins, he gripped them tightly and stepped in toward the horse, which backed away halfheartedly. Slocum moved in tight and patted the horse, talking quietly to calm it down. When the animal seemed no longer frightened, he led it back toward the creek.

He tethered the horse, with its English saddle, to some brush and walked back to the bank. Wrestling Moseley's body into his arms, he struggled toward the horse and hoisted the corpse over the saddle. There was no lariat to tie the body on with, and he had to walk back to his own horse for some rope.

It looked like the Double Rocker would have to get along without him for another day.

10

Dry Spring loomed up out of the sun-bright haze like a desert mirage. Behind him, Slocum heard the steady clop of the second horse. He tried to push its burden out of his mind, but there was no getting away from it. He kept his own mount moving at a steady pace, and the follow horse was content to go along, occasionally tugging on the reins looped over Slocum's saddle horn.

At the left edge of the town, Clayton Ramsey's colorful tent stood out like a beacon. Its red stripes were half bleached by the bright sun to a dark pink. The white stripes sparkled like freshly broken bone. Slocum dreaded the thought of telling the old man what had happened, but he knew he had to do it. Better from him than the sheriff. In spite of himself, he realized he was speeding up as the town drew closer. He wanted it over with, and his mount seemed to know it.

When he reached the outlying buildings, the street was empty, but as he entered the town limits, he realized someone must have seen him. He heard a shout behind him, and someone else responded. He turned to see people spilling out into the street behind him, as if he were a circus come to town.

The sheriff's office was on the other end of Dry Spring, three blocks away. Three blocks that seemed a continent. He thought it would never end. The shouting continued, and more people joined the crowd. By the time he'd covered the last block, twenty or thirty people stood in the street, watching from a distance. They talked to one another as if they'd never seen a dead man before. And maybe they hadn't—not dead this way, anyhow.

Slocum dismounted and tied off at the hitching post. He unwrapped the reins of the second horse, knotted them loosely around the post, and turned as he heard someone shout his name.

Pete Harney waddled across the street. "Slocum, what the hell is going on?" he shouted.

Slocum cocked a thumb over his shoulder toward the body. "Your guess is as good as mine, Pete."

"What happened? He fall and break his neck?"

"I wish that was it, Pete."

He turned to the boardwalk and climbed up, Harney right behind him. The door of the sheriff's office was open. The room beyond was full of shade. He stepped to the doorway, his spurs clinking the only sound. Poking his head in, he called, "Sheriff? You in there?"

"Who wants to know?"

Movement in the back room, followed by a bulky shadow in the doorway leading to the office, interrupted the answer.

"I do," Slocum said. "Sheriff, you better come on outside."

"Who the hell are you?"

"Name's Slocum, John Slocum."

Ray Castle was a big man, and his voice sounded like empty barrels rolling around the hold of a ship, booming in the small space. "You from around here? Don't think I've had the pleasure."

"He's a new man at the Double Rocker, Ray," Harney volunteered.

"That so? Well, Slocum, you mind telling me what's so damned important I ought to step out in that infernal sun?"

"Somebody's been shot, Sheriff."

"Hell, you want Doc Chambliss, then."

"No need for the doc, Ray. The man's dead. Shot dead."

Castle looked at Harney for a long minute. "Well, Pete, since you seem to know so much about it, maybe you ought to tell me who done the killing. How about it?"

"Sorry, Sheriff," Harney said. "Just trying to help's all."

Castle stepped around his desk and moved past Slocum toward the door. He stood in the doorway for a long moment, then turned to Slocum. In the shadows, it was hard to see his features. He said, "Yep, man sure looks dead to me. Who is he?"

"His name was Moseley," Slocum said. "He worked in that theater group came into town a couple of days ago."

"I guess I better have a look." Castle stepped on through the door, and Slocum followed him out onto the boardwalk. Stepping into the street, the sheriff towered over Slocum's mount. He stepped between the horses after circling the rail, and looked at the body. He was squinting in the bright sun, but other than that his face betrayed nothing.

"Think I saw this feller this morning. Backshot, looks like to me." He turned to Slocum. "You see it happen?"

"No sir. He was already dead when I found him, out toward the Double Rocker."

Castle acted as if he hadn't heard. He turned to Harney. "Pete, you want to run down to McIntyre's and have him come get this fellow?"

"Sure thing, Ray."

To Slocum, the sheriff said, "Suppose we go on inside and you tell me what happened, alright? Far as you know, anyhow . . ." He waited to watch Harney hurry up the street, waved his hand at the small knot of people milling around twenty yards away, and shouted, "Show's over, folks. Go on about your business."

Castle stepped back onto the boardwalk and reentered his office. When Slocum followed, the sheriff was already sitting behind his desk, his boots up on the scarred top. "Have a seat, Mr. Slocum."

Sitting down in the only other chair, Slocum winced, and inhaled sharply.

"You're the feller had that run-in with Brett Mackay over to Harney's, ain't you?"

"Yup."

"Mackay's a puzzlement. He gets a few drinks in him, he can go hog-wild. I heard somebody jumped you, but you didn't see who it was. That right?"

"Pretty much."

"Well, don't blame it on Dry Spring, Slocum. You find Mackay and his kind everyplace you go. I ought to know. I been sheriff just about everyplace the last twenty-five years." He paused to light a cigarette from a small bowl on the desk. He nodded toward the bowl. "Light up, if you feel like it."

"Not with these ribs, but thanks."

"Suit yourself. Now, suppose you tell me exactly what you saw."

Slocum filled him in as best he could, and Castle listened without interruption. When he was done, he spread his hands, palms up. "And that's really all I can tell you."

"And you say you didn't recognize them men you saw hightailing it across the ridge, that right?"

"Right. Like I said, I don't even know if they're connected. I didn't hear a shot—not that I would have necessarily. But I didn't. And Moseley hadn't been dead more than a half hour before I found him, give or take."

"You sure about that?"

"Sure as I can be. The blood was still wet on his shirt. The bugs hadn't started on him yet, and it doesn't usually take them too long."

"And how'd you happen to find him, again?"

"Like I told you, I was on the way back to the Double Rocker. The ride was a little more than I thought, and I wanted to get a drink and some shade, rest up some, before pushing on."

"Sure wish to hell you'd got a good look at them cowboys. Not that I think they had anything to do with it necessarily. But it would be nice to be able to ask them personal."

"Anything I can do, Sheriff, you let me know."

"You going back to the ranch?"

"Not today. I better spend another day or two in town. I'll be at the Dry Spring Hotel, you want to talk to me again."

"Oh, I will, Mr. Slocum. I surely will. I think it only fair to warn you, all I got is what you give me. For all I know, it was you killed the fancy boy. You mind lettin' me take a look at your sidearm?"

Slocum looked annoyed, and Castle noticed. "Now, don't take it personal, Slocum. I got a job here. Far as I know, you're the last one seen the man alive. I know you said he was already dead, but that's what you say, not what I know." He took the Colt and sniffed the barrel. "Nice piece of work. Don't see too many of these here Colts no more. Seems like everybody wants a Peacemaker."

Slocum took the gun and holstered it.

"Satisfied, Sheriff?" he asked.

"Should I be? Man's still dead. And I still don't know who killed him. That don't satisfy me, Mr. Slocum, no sir, it surely don't. For what it's worth, I don't think you killed him, though."

"Thanks for that, at least."

"But I would appreciate it if you'd stop by before you go back out to Tim Baker's spread. If it's no trouble."

Slocum shook his head. "No trouble."

"Good. I'll see you around then, I guess."

Slocum stood up to leave. As he walked to the door, Castle called after him, "Slocum?" He turned, and Castle nodded. "Thanks. You could have left him there, I know. Lot of men would've."

Slocum walked out into the street. A few stragglers watched as he untied his horse. Instead of mounting up, he tugged the chestnut along behind him to the livery stable. The heat was oppressive, and he was exhausted. The stableman stood out front as he approached.

"Thought you was going back to work."

"So did I."

"You still got two days comin' on your week. No charge."

"Thanks, old-timer."

"Course, you insist on callin' me old-timer, I might forget about that balance and bill you again."

Slocum was too weary to grin. The faint smile died almost as soon as it appeared.

"Rough day, son?"

Slocum nodded.

"You be at the same hotel?"

"Yep."

"Make sure they give you a room with a door," he cackled.

"Heard about that, did you?"

"Dry Spring don't have too much news, son. Somethin' like that helps pass the time. You know how it is."

Slocum allowed as how he did, indeed, know how it was. But he was too worn out to let the old man know how little he sympathized with that boredom. All he wanted was a bath and a bed. And he'd pass on the bath if he could only have one of the two. With every step up the dusty street, he thought less about the bath and more about sleep. By the time he reached the hotel, all he could think of was something soft to lie down on.

The clerk looked surprised to see him. "Back so soon?"

"You got a room, I hope."

"Oh, yes sir, Mr. Slocum."

He signed in and had to reach twice for the key before catching it with his fingertips. By the time he got to the head of the stairs, he was tempted to lie on the floor and go to sleep right there. He stumbled down to his room, got the door open, and fell into bed.

He smelled the clean sheets and lay there with his eyes closed, trying to remember whether he had locked the door behind him. When he realized he hadn't, he also realized he didn't care. He needed sleep.

He thought about Ramsey, but he just couldn't do it. He would see the old man later, if the sheriff didn't get there first. And if he did, maybe it would be for the best.

11

It was dark when Slocum woke up. He sat on the bed for a long time, and finally decided to light the lamp. He groped around in the dark, found the chimney, and lifted it. He struck a match with his thumbnail and set the wick. The chimney clattered back into place, and somehow the room seemed a little less dreary, bathed in the soft orange glow.

Only too aware of the stale stench of sweat, he pulled off his shirt and unwrapped the bandages binding his ribs. His skin was all puckered from the tape, puffed into ridges at either side. The ugly purple had faded to a yellow-green even uglier. His mouth felt like the floor of a barn, and tasted like what he imagined a barn floor to taste like.

One of the few virtues of the Dry Spring Hotel was indoor plumbing. He needed a bath, and he didn't give a damn how late it was.

The bathroom was down the hall, and he lugged his shaving gear and a change of clothes down the carpeted corridor. He locked the door behind him. A single lamp, its wick turned well down, glimmered faintly from the solitary sconce high on the wall. Slocum turned on the tap and listened to the dull plash of water, the rumble in the pipes. The cold was easy, running down from a tank on the roof. The hot was less cooperative. It spat and chattered on the way up from a boiler in the basement.

When the big enameled claw-foot was three-quarters full, he stripped off his pants and underwear and lowered himself into the water. The brown soap was anything but cosmetic, but right now he needed clean, not pretty.

He lay there a long time, listening to his heartbeat. Half submerged, the noise in his ears sounded like mountains falling apart, as if the planet were about to break up. It was eerie, but strangely peaceful. With his eyes closed, he concentrated on the steady rumble. Holding himself as still as possible, he wanted to hear nothing but the incessant rhythm, rock solid, as predictable as life was impossible to predict. It made the future seem a little more secure. Nothing that powerful, that insistent, could be denied.

Or so he wanted to believe.

When the water started to cool, he soaped himself briskly, then ducked under, dousing his head again and working the harsh brown soap into a thin film in his hair. Rinsing, he did it again, and scratched at his beard, trying to soften it for the coming razor.

He climbed out carefully, wrapped a towel around his waist, and worked the shaving brush into a full lather. Smearing the thick foam on his whiskers, he relaxed again, letting the warmth soak into him as if it were pure energy. He felt refreshed, even cheerful as he scratched away at the growth of several days. The razor began to dull, and he scraped even harder, determined to wash away every last vestige of the past few days.

For a moment, Slocum felt like a new man. But as he backed away, rubbing the reddened skin of his jaw, he caught a glimpse of his ribs in the fogged-over mirror. The bruises were still there, just as Brett Mackay was still there, and Moseley was still dead. Some things you just couldn't wash away.

Slocum slipped into clean clothes, glad finally to be free of the constraints of the bandages. He rinsed the tub down, gathered his laundry and shaving gear, and walked back down the hall, feeling less and less like a new man with every step. The invigoration of the bath hadn't lasted long. He felt the same cloud of depression, the same gloom, begin to swirl around him, and he wondered how he could have been so simpleminded as to think things could have changed so easily.

Back in his room, he sat in a chair and stared at the bed, the laundry still in his lap. The clothes smelled of death, but he couldn't place it at first. Then he remembered Moseley, and hoisting the body onto the horse. He tossed the old clothes to the floor, kicking them away with a bare foot. In the morning, he'd have to burn them.

And it wasn't over yet. He wanted to talk to Clayton Ramsey. The old man seemed to have bottomed out in Dry Spring. Things were happening all around him. Whether it was because of him or not, Ramsey seemed to be a lightning rod of sorts, attracting all manner of bad luck. Slocum thought about his own father, how another old man used to sit him on his knee and talk to him about everything from history to the Bible. Right now, history wasn't much help, and the Bible never had seemed very real to him. But this was one of those times when he wished he could believe. It must be nice to have something to turn to, something to believe in, when there seemed no reason to believe in anything at all.

Slocum remembered the story of Job, and wondered

whether Clayton Ramsey was another victim of the same cruel game. The trouble was, you had to believe in God to believe he would waste his time playing games with the devil. And what a strange God that would be. Somehow, it was better not to believe at all than to believe in a God like that. He knew his father would be outraged at such a thought, but the son had seen so much that the father could only imagine.

The knock on the door sounded far away, as if from another floor of the hotel. He stared at the closed door, not even sure he'd heard it. Again, this time more insistently, someone rapped. This time, he was sure.

Getting to his feet, grateful for the intrusion, but not a little resentful at being dragged out of his mood, he crossed the floor slowly. At the door, he paused with a hand on the lock. When the visitor knocked a third time, he unlocked the door and pulled it open.

He glanced at the gunbelt coiled on the night table, cursing himself for being so far from the gun. But the woman who entered seemed harmless enough.

"How are you, Mr. Slocum?"

"Portia?"

"You recognized me! How nice of you."

"What do you want?"

"That's rather ungracious, don't you think?"

"I'm feeling rather ungracious, actually. I'd apologize, but that wouldn't be ungracious, so I guess it would be out of character at the moment."

" 'Would you care to sit down, Portia?' 'Why yes, thank you for asking.' That's how it's supposed to go, Mr. Slocum."

He ignored the sarcasm and watched her as she glanced around the room. "Oh my, I'm not . . . interrupting anything, am I?"

"No."

She smiled then. Dropping into the only chair, she watched him until he grew uncomfortable under her gaze.

He turned away. Walking across the room, he turned the lamp up.

"Oh, do turn it down, please. Hotel rooms are so dreary. Don't you think so?"

"Never thought about it."

"What do you think about, Mr. Slocum?"

"As little as possible."

She got up slowly and walked to the door. He thought his chilly reception might have warned her off. But instead, she turned the lock and walked over to the bed, patting the mattress idly with her fingertips. "Quite comfortable, are you?"

"I've been worse off."

"I'll bet you have." She walked toward the lamp and snicked the wick all the way down. The light went out, leaving an afterimage of its guttering orange flame. Then that, too, was gone.

He heard the springs creak as she sat on the bed. Then, he heard her hand patting the mattress. "Sit down, Mr. Slocum. I think you need some cheering up."

Slocum ignored her. He heard the rustle of cloth in the darkness, then felt her hand on his hip. Carefully, she slid her fingers up along his ribs. "Still tender, aren't they?"

He murmured assent, and when she tugged on his belt, he didn't resist. Sitting on the edge of the bed, he felt distant, almost absent. She moved again, the springs creaking under the movement. Her fingers tangled themselves in his still-damp hair, brushing stray locks back away from his forehead. Then, gently but insistently, she tugged him down until he lay across the bed. She took his hand and placed it on her own hip.

The cool, smooth skin under his fingers told him everything she wanted him to know. He seemed indifferent, letting his hand lie on the curve of her hip, motionless and inert. She was on her knees, and leaned over him, her hands cupping his face like a precious thing, something she was afraid to break. He couldn't see in the dark, but sensed her body coming closer, then something brushed his lips. Smooth, even ripe, he realized it was a breast. A nipple, stiff and erect, teased him until his lips parted, and then it was gone.

Her fingers worried the buttons of his shirt. She stripped it open, careful of his tender ribs, and her lips, cool and smooth as silk, traced first one then another and a third of his battered bones. Her hair cascaded across his chest, its fragrance swirling around him. He inhaled it like a breath of fresh air. For the first time, his hands moved on their own and he piled the curls around him, trying to forget the stench of Moseley's corpse that still clung to him, at least in his own mind.

Portia said something he didn't hear, then her lips brushed against his ear. Her tongue darted in, tickling him, and he tried to move away, laughing in spite of himself. Again he sensed her hovering over him, and this time the full breast didn't tease. Greedily, he sucked it in, his tongue circling the pebbled aureole. The nipple, hard and getting harder, between his teeth, he moved his head from side to side, then opened his mouth to swallow as much of her as he could.

"Mmmm," she said, "I think you're cheering up a little."

She pulled away and pressed the breast against his cheek. He felt his slickness on the smooth skin, and sought the other breast. She unbuckled his dungarees and he raised his hips while she stripped them off, then his underwear. Even in the hot night air his skin felt suddenly cold.

Her hand closed over him, and he moaned, raising himself again to follow the gliding silk of her hand. Squeezing, then stroking, she teased him erect. She seemed to vanish for a moment, then he felt her weight surround him, the gentle prod of her nipples as she bent to kiss him. Her tongue traced the curve of his lower lip, her teeth nibbled at it, then her tongue again, sliding inside him to meet his own. He sucked on it more eagerly than he had the breast.

Again, her fingers curled around his erection, this time

guiding him. He felt the dampness of her as she rubbed it against her. She pulled away, and for a moment he thought she was getting up. Then, so suddenly it took his breath away, she took him inside, lowering herself along the full length of him, then slipping away again. Slowly, fraction by fraction, she drew him in. The noise of her wetness, crackling like fire, echoed in the darkness.

He felt the heat of her, then the press of her as she started to move. Slowly up, slowly down, more slowly and then a frenzy of movement ending in a moment of perfect motionlessness, balanced on the edge of something. He raised his hips, but she pressed him back down with spread fingers. Again and again, she took that long, shuddering ride down the length of him, and with every descent he tried harder to move, but she was in total control.

He listened in the dark to the sound of his cock cresting through the sea of her, felt her juices trickle down between his legs. He moved inside her in spite of himself, and in spite of her, straining up as she backed away. Then, with a sound deep in her throat like the growl of an angry cougar, she moved faster. His hands rested on her hips, slick with sweat. The ripe scent of her broke over him in waves as she moved still faster. She threw her head back, her hair lashing at his legs as she swung from side to side.

The snarl turned to a moan as he slid his hands up along her ribs and cupped her breasts, his thumbs teasing in small circles around the hard nipples. She was moving now with a kind of recklessness almost beyond rhythm, and she let him match her, falling in step with the last frenzied moments of her wild ride. He felt their sweat-slickened skins sliding together, heard the sucking of her thighs on every stroke, and he drove up and in, deeper and deeper, until she cried out.

She seemed to collapse, no longer careful of his injury, letting her breasts crush against his chest. He grabbed fistfuls of her hair and buried his face in the fragrant curls. He lay still for a long minute, conscious of the insistent hardness still buried deep inside her. She twitched her hips and he started to move again, this time in easy rhythm.

But she backed away. The shock of the night air, after the heat of her, made him go limp.

"We have to talk," she said, lying beside him.

He rubbed the tangled thatch between her legs, letting his fingers just graze the damp lips beyond it. "I'm listening."

12

"Alright, I've done you a favor, now I want to ask you for one."

Slocum felt as if he'd been slapped. He had heard the words clearly. There was no question of having misunderstood her. But could she be that openly mercenary?

"Why should I do you a favor?" he asked.

"You think I came here just to go to bed with you? Don't kid yourself, Slocum. It wasn't that special."

"I didn't think so either. But it was worth the money it cost."

He felt her twist away from him in the dark. He thought for a moment she was getting up. But she twisted back and smacked him, hard, across the face. It stung as much from surprise as from the blow itself. "You bastard," she hissed.

He lay there quietly, thinking she might leave, and hoping she would. This time, she surprised him. Her body pressed against him, and she kissed the same cheek. Her lips felt hot, even feverish on the stinging flesh. "I'm sorry," she said. "I didn't mean that. It's just that . . . " She trailed off. Draping a long leg over his legs, she slid in even closer.

"Do you have any idea what my life is like, Slocum? Traveling from town to town like some damn Gypsy, making friends and leaving them, all in a week. Seeing someplace you fall in love with, then watching it disappear over your shoulder. I've been a thousand places, some of them paradise and some of them hell, but I never got to know a single one of them."

"Why do you do it?"

"Because it's the only thing I've ever done. Because my father loves it, I guess, and because I love my father."

"Those are not bad reasons." He found himself feeling sorry for her, in spite of himself. "But, yes, I do know what it's like not having a home. At least you have a family, people you love and trust, right there with you. That has to count for something, doesn't it?"

"Yes and no." She shifted on the bed, turning on her stomach and draping an arm across his chest, then resting her head on his shoulder. "It's better than not having family, I guess. But having them only gives you more to worry about. Slocum, John, you have to understand, this is killing my father, but he won't admit it. Maybe he doesn't even realize it. I don't know, but I know it's killing him. He's too old for this kind of life."

"Maybe you have to let him be the judge of that. Maybe he loves it enough that it compensates for all the rest."

"For him, maybe." Her breath was hot in his ear, her voice a murmur, not seductive, more confiding, as if, having bared her body to him, shown him everything else, she had no choice but to bare her soul, too.

Conscious of her body in a new way, he hoisted her up, gently, and let her down full length on top of him. He felt a stirring in his groin, but he ignored it. Tenderly, with one hand, he stroked her back, running his fingertips along her spine, from the nape of her neck to the cleft of her ass, and back. Her body felt good against his. It was good weight pressing him into the bed.

"Why don't you give it up," Slocum asked, "lead your own life, one you can be happy with?"

"I can't leave my father. It would kill him."

"Maybe not. Maybe he'd welcome it."

"How could you even think that? It's all he's done for fifty years. It's the only thing he knows. Bundling his family into those goddamn wagons and looking for the next town big enough to play. My mother took sick in one of these hick towns. She died in another. I can't even visit her grave." She grew profoundly quiet. Only her breathing broke the silence. It was shallow and uneven, as if she struggled to keep something inside.

Slocum waited, stroking her hair like a concerned parent, and when she regained some control, he said, "Sometimes we do things we don't want to do. We've been doing them so long, we don't know how to stop. But sometimes we do them because we think it's what other people want us to do. People who matter to us, family, whatever. We do it for them, and never stop to consider whether we even know *what* they want. Maybe that's what the professor is doing."

"Don't call him that." She pulled away for a moment. "He's no more a professor than you are. It's just another role. He's always on stage. Even in the damn wagons, out in the middle of nowhere, he's performing. If he's not rehearsing some lines, he's pretending to be something he's not. You don't understand at all. There *is* no person under all that tomfoolery. None. He's a figment of his own imagination, a character in a play he's been writing all his life."

"If you cared about him, you would have told *him* that, not me."

"You think I haven't? You think he'd listen? Oh no, not the Great Professor Clayton Ramsey. He listens only to Shakespeare and to God. His equals, you see. That's who he listens to. It was different when my mother was alive. He trusted her judgment. She knew how to handle him, and he let her do it. He *wanted* to be handled. But now . . . everybody has an axe to grind. Cordelia wants him to keep doing just what he's doing. Since he can't make a decision, he does what she tells him, because she tells him just what he wants to hear. And Juliet, well . . . I don't want to talk about that. . . . "

She rested her head on his shoulder again, her lips pressed against the hollow of his throat. Slocum felt the trickle of a tear run over his shoulder and lose itself in the bedding. He caressed her, his hands disconnected from his body. Aware of her smooth skin, but not reacting to her flesh. She wiggled her hips to get more comfortable and heaved a sigh.

"What can I do about any of this, Portia? He doesn't know me from Adam."

"Maybe you can't do anything. But at least you can try. Slocum, you don't understand what it's like. That man who attacked him. There's a man like that in nearly every town. Something in my father brings out the worst in them. He's an old man, Slocum, an old man who doesn't have the sense he was born with. He doesn't see it, and if he does, he doesn't understand. One day one of those men will kill him, or hurt him so badly, maybe even cripple him, that it will amount to the same thing."

"I can't be a bodyguard for him, if that's what you're suggesting."

"No, that's not what I'm suggesting. All I want is for you to talk to him, try to explain to him how dangerous all this is."

"You want me to talk the man into giving up his whole

life. Is that all? You want me to talk him into cutting off an arm or a leg while I'm at it? That's what it would amount to. I can't do that. Besides, Cordelia is concerned about him. So are you. You're his family. It's your right, but I don't have that right. Even if you ask, I don't have that right."

"But you have to. You owe it to him."

Slocum was stunned. "I *owe* it to him. What on earth for?"

"You protected him, maybe even saved his life the other night. You're responsible for him now. You interfered, and you have to accept the responsibility. Don't you see, he'll think you were meant to be there, meant to save him. It's always like that. He won't accept that it was just blind luck, an accident, chance, whatever you want to call it. He just won't. But you can make him see that. You can talk some sense into him."

"What sort of sense? What can I possibly tell him that would matter?"

"You can convince him to sell. He's had offers, lots of them. But he's too stubborn. He won't even talk to anyone interested in buying the theater."

"Then he won't listen to me. And there's no reason he should. I don't know anything about the theater. How can I ask a man to sell something when I don't know what it's worth? How can I ask a man I don't even know to sell his life to the highest bidder?"

"Won't you just try?"

"No."

"Please? Slocum, please?"

He was wavering, and she knew it. And she read him too well to ask again. Her silence was more persuasive than anything she could say. He lay there quietly, conscious of her body, of her heat. He could hear his heart pounding in his ears, and felt hers pounding in her chest. He put his hands on her hips to shift her weight, then let them slide down to rest on her ass, the firm cheeks and cool skin so inviting, so tempting. And he knew he was being tempted, but not why, or even to do what.

"Let me think about it," he said.

"I suppose that's fair."

She wiggled her hips again, pressing her body down tightly against him, and this time he couldn't ignore the stirring. She felt it too, and her legs opened slowly. With a hand on either side of his head, she raised herself until she could slide off him.

She lay on her back and reached for him, tracing his ribs with her fingers, scoring broad circles on his aching chest, then raking her nails down along the center of his body. Playfully tugging at the hair between his legs, she pulled him toward her. He felt her legs spread wider. She found the erection, closed it in her fist, and guided him atop her.

When he entered her, she moaned, then curled her long legs around him, stroking his calves with the soles of her feet. Wide open to him, she settled back and let him find his rhythm, taking his every cue. Her hips rocked against him, hard when he rocked hard, gently when he held back. He was calling the shots this time.

When he finished and lay still, panting on her chest, he said, "I don't even know what you look like, I mean like this."

"Does it matter, Slocum?"

"No. It doesn't matter."

Carefully extricating herself, she slid off the bed. He heard the clink of glass on metal, then saw a spurt of orange flame. At first, his eyes accustomed to the darkness, he saw just a silhouette. As they adjusted to the dim light, she turned and came back to the bed. Her breasts were fuller than he imagined, dark aureoles perched just at the upturn. Her legs were long and slender, giving no hint of their strength, their suppleness. The auburn thatch, darker than the jumbled curls around her shoulders, was a perfect triangle. But it was the face that stunned him.

The lean, almost carnivorous cast of their first meeting was gone. In repose, her features were softer, fuller, less voracious.

"Now you have," she said. "Does it make a difference?"

He shook his head.

She lay down again beside him, stretching full length. Luxuriantly, she reached high above her head and took a deep breath. He rolled on one hip, but couldn't bring himself to touch her. She seemed so perfectly formed, so fragile despite the strength of her, that he thought she might break, or that it might be a sin of some sort, even a sacrilege. He wanted to say something, tell her how beautiful she was. But he knew it would sound foolish, and he knew, too, that it would not come as news to her. Every curve of her body, every ripple of muscle under the satin skin, made his heart pound a little harder.

But he couldn't touch her. Not again, not now.

She brought her arms down, and, half sitting up, she looked at him for the first time since coming back to bed. She smiled, then leaned over and kissed him. It was so chaste, it felt like a sister's kiss.

"Thank you," she said.

"For what?"

"For talking to my father."

"I didn't say I would talk to him."

"But you will." She sat on the edge of the bed, smiling. "You will."

"Yes," he said. "I will."

13

Portia left before dawn. Slocum watched the door close, then lay awake. Over and over, he tried to frame his approach to Clayton Ramsey. But no matter how he reworked it, it came out wrong. He knew he was going to be wasting his time. He wasn't even sure why he was going to try. He didn't owe Portia a thing, not really. She had asked and he had, reluctantly, agreed.

And he didn't know why.

That, more than anything else, was what troubled him. He felt like an intruder. What gave him the right to poke into another man's life, question his dreams, tell him it was all over, that he should take to the pasture and thank his lucky stars? And he made no mistake about it, that's exactly what he'd be doing. Meddling didn't sit easily on his shoulders.

It wasn't how he was raised. It wasn't how he was made.

So why, he kept wondering, was he going to do it? But he knew the answer. He was going to do it because Portia was right. Clayton Ramsey was vulnerable as only the old can be vulnerable. Unwilling to face the fact of their diminishing capacity, unable to admit that there were other, younger, people who could do what they no longer could and, worse still, who *should* do it.

More than that, he realized, was at work in him. He hadn't been able to help his own father. Maybe, by helping Ramsey, he could alleviate some of that guilt. Maybe he could atone for that failure somehow. He knew, at least, that he had to try.

He got no sleep. The ceiling slowly materialized as the sun neared the edge of the world. The first gray blades speared past the drapes, smeared themselves on the wall, leaving shadows from the wallpaper's flocked pattern. It looked to Slocum like some foreign language, a message he couldn't understand but couldn't ignore.

As the day cracked open, and brighter light seeped around the drapes like blood oozing from a knife wound, he started to grow restless. The room still carried the scent of Portia, small pockets of fragrance that swirled around him unexpectedly each time a breeze muscled its way past the heavy drapery.

Slocum was trapped, and he knew it. A prisoner of his own good intentions. Coloring it all, fueling his willingness, was his anger at Brett Mackay. Portia was right about the cowboy. Maybe not personally, but about his type. Men like Mackay were a dime a dozen, and they never picked on a John Slocum when a Clayton Ramsey was handy. Targets of opportunity, they had called it in the war. If it moves, blow a hole in it. You're a soldier, and that's what you do. When you're a bully, it's a little simpler: if you can beat it, and it can't beat you, take it on.

What Slocum wanted, deep down inside, was another crack at Brett Mackay. It galled him to realize how selfish he was being. But then Portia had been selfish, too. She wanted something from him, something she didn't have, and she used her body to get it. Slocum smiled grimly wondering whether she would have been so free with herself if she had known he would have done her bidding for free. He didn't really want to know, but he couldn't help wondering.

He suspected, even half believed, that Portia was just using him, and he knew he should just take what she was willing to give, without investing anything of himself. That's what he knew, what he felt was more complicated than that.

When the early sun had bled away, turned to orange, then yellow, and finally a brilliant white, he sat up on the bed. His clothes still lay on the floor where Portia had thrown them. He stared at them a moment, remembering how they came to be there, then pulled them on, a piece at a time.

Dressed, he sat down again, pulled the Colt Navy from its holster, and cracked it open. He jerked every shell free, cupped them in his hands like dice, and dumped them on the pillow, where their weight kept them in a small hollow. The gun was clean, but he cleaned it again. The sharp tang of the oil seemed to heighten his awareness, made him tense. Ramming each shell back into the cylinder, it dawned on him that he was thinking ahead unconsciously. By no stretch of the imagination would he need the gun to deal with Clayton Ramsey, but he was looking beyond that. It was as if he already knew what Ramsey's answer would be. And that meant he'd have to deal with Brett Mackay.

Finally, when he was finished with the gun, as if some ritual had been satisfactorily completed, he strapped on the gunbelt and stepped into the hall. The hotel was still quiet. At seven o'clock, that was no surprise. Down in the lobby, he nodded to the clerk and opened the front door. It was one of those late-summer days when there is more light than heat before noon. Everything looked sharp and bright. On the boardwalk in front of the hotel he could see every edge sharply etched, every angle clearly defined.

At the far end of town, the red and white tent loomed over everything like a monument commemorating nothing. He dropped to the dusty street and started toward the theater. His spurs made the only sound. A dog barked once, out on the edge of town, then whimpered and was still. As he walked down the center of the street, the windows on the west side caught the sun, still low on the horizon, flashing like gun barrels across a valley floor.

He wondered whether Ramsey was up at this early hour, whether he was being overanxious. Part of him didn't want to waste time with Ramsey at all, wanted to get right down to the bone. But there was a logic to events, one he couldn't ignore, anymore than Ramsey could ignore Shakespeare's lines if he wanted to play Lear.

As he drew close, Slocum noticed the tent was anything but quiet. The entrance was on the far side, and he could hear shouting, only faintly muffled by the canvas, from inside. Several dull thuds echoed up through the small opening around the pole, and Ramsey's voice, apparently amplified by something, thundered at all and sundry.

Slocum picked up his pace. There was something in Ramsey that attracted him, like a lodestone drawing iron filings to itself. The man had presence. He was loud, a bit of a buffoon even, but there was something special about him that couldn't be denied. You could ignore it, but that wouldn't make it go away.

He turned the corner and bumped into Cordelia, nearly knocking her down. "Morning, ma'am," he said, touching his fingers to the brim of his hat. She glared at him, then swept around him without a word. He stared after her, baffled by the chilly reception. Ramsey spotted him before he'd fully recovered.

"Mr. Slocum, how are you? Come to see the troupers at play, have you?"

"Morning, Professor."

"Come, come, man. No need to stand on ceremony. You did me a great service, sir. I am in your debt."

The words seemed to thunder from his lips the way water thundered over Niagara. There was bluster—it seemed Ramsey was incapable of suppressing it—but there was genuine pleasure in the greeting, as well.

"What can I do for you, Mr. Slocum? Just name it. Anything but Cordelia's hand in holy matrimony. That I shall have to deny you. So, unless you've come to plight your troth to my youngest, you have but to name your pleasure and you shall have it. Freely given."

"Not hardly the marrying kind, Professor. I just thought I'd come by and see how you're doing."

" 'Twas nothing, son, nothing. A knock on this old head can do no harm, none at all."

"I wasn't so sure. You seemed to be pretty badly shaken up."

"I am used to it, Mr. Slocum. Past master of dealing with the likes of that ruffian. But I hear you suffered rather more at his hand than I. I apologize for not coming to see you. I fully intended, but, the press of business, you see . . . we open tonight. *Macbeth*. May I impose on you to attend?"

"I'm not much of a theatergoer, Professor. I—"

"Nonsense, *non*sense. You're an intelligent young man. That's all you need to appreciate the Immortal Bard at his finest."

"Alright, I'll try."

"Feeling rather better, are you? I trust Cordelia conveyed my thanks. I sent her, you know."

"Yes, she said so. It wasn't necessary."

"You seem preoccupied, Mr. Slocum. Anything I can do?"

"Actually, I would like a few words with you. Alone, if that's possible."

"Yes, of course I—Look out, you lunkheads, that flat took a week to paint." Ramsey stormed past him, toward the low stage where several young men were attempting to assemble a set for the evening's performance. They scattered as he charged, calling down all sorts of punishment for every conceivable sort of dereliction, from bastardy to just plain stupidity.

Slocum shook his head, only half believing the man could have so much energy. Watching him assail the crew, it was hard to believe that Cordelia could feel him threatened by anything, or Portia could believe him too old to carry on his business. Backing away, only half satisfied, Ramsey continued to rail at the half-dozen crew members until he was back at Slocum's side.

"I suppose I must intimidate them, but I mean no harm. I think they know that. But you have no idea how precarious an existence a theater such as ours must endure. I have had a dozen wagons burned over the years, twice by rampaging red men. I have been shot at with minié balls and arrows and slingshots, had horses stolen, actresses kidnapped. It's a wonder I've managed to keep it together this long. And now, this awful business with young Moseley . . . " He shook his head sadly. "I warned him, of course, many times. Told him he should be careful. It's a burden, you know, not being like other men. But it's an awful thing that happened, all the same."

"Actually, Professor, that's what I wanted to talk to you about."

"Oh?"

"Yes sir, I was wondering whether you've had any more trouble from Brett Mackay."

"Don't know the man. Unless . . . ah, I see, the malefactor we have in common, eh? No, I've not seen him since our initial encounter. Don't expect I will, either."

"That's not what I've been hearing."

"If you mean my daughter has tried to frighten you on my behalf, ignore it."

"No sir, that's not what I mean. Can we talk? Please?"

"Of course, of course. Come with me to my wagon. Let's away." He bowed low, sweeping the ground with his hat, like some courtier. Slocum just shook his head, not knowing whether to laugh or feel sorry for the old man.

Ramsey took him by the sleeve, tugging him back out of the tent. "Come on, come on. You want to talk, let's go talk."

Cordelia sat on the steps of her wagon. She stared at Slocum with a kind of distant look, as if she weren't quite conscious. Slocum watched her as Ramsey pulled him on by, leading the way to his own wagon.

Once inside, he turned on a lamp. "You care for a drink, Mr. Slocum? I have some very fine brandy. It's a bit early, but we actors have a different sense of time."

Slocum shook his head, and Ramsey recapped the crystal decanter without pouring himself a drink. Dropping into a small chair, he said, "Now, what's on your mind?"

"Well, I don't know quite how to put this."

"Just blurt it out, that's all."

Slocum nodded. "Alright. I've been hearing things, talk, rumors, you know how it is in a small town."

"You're worried about Mackay, aren't you?"

"Yes, I suppose I am."

"Don't be. I've seen his type before. All noise and no sense at all. He was just a little too drunk and a little too full of himself. He meant me no harm. I suspect he meant you none, either. When you live as long as I have, you can see through all the smoke, son. Don't worry about Brett Mackay."

"It's more than that. It's Moseley, too. I think Mackay had something to do with that."

"So the sheriff said. But he also said you couldn't say for sure. You didn't really see anything. I guess it's natural, after the scrape you had with him, to blame him for everything. But sometimes things just happen. Moseley was a good lad. I miss him, and I mourn for him. But . . . " Ramsey spread his arms, shrugging helplessly. "It's not the first time I've lost one of my troupe. They're not so conventional, you know. In fact, we've had another defection. Louis Marillac this time. But people do what they have to do. They don't always say goodbye. As far as Moseley is concerned, well . . . who knows?"

"What makes you so sure Mackay didn't do it?"

"Sure? I'm not sure. Not at all. But I can't see the point of worrying about a man who may or may not have done something. If I knew, I would spring the trapdoor under him myself, and sit on his shoulders on the way down. But I'm not sure, and life is too complex and too damn short, son. Brooding gets you nowhere. If you believe, then you act. If you suspect, you have no choice but to wait and see. Shakespeare teaches us that. Hamlet, you see, that was his problem. He wasn't sure. People criticize the play, say Hamlet is indecisive. Not fair. Not true. He was prudent, he wanted to know, to be sure. Only then does a wise man act. Not before."

"You're too generous, Professor, too fair-minded, maybe."

"No such thing, son."

"Have you ever thought about retiring, maybe selling the theater?"

"Ah, I see Portia's hand in this. Whatever for? What would I do then? What *could* I do? I think I would die. The theater is what I live for, Mr. Slocum. That and my children. And the theater is the only thing I have to leave them. If I were to sell it, I would die unhappy, a failure, and a traitor to my children."

Slocum sat back, relieved that Ramsey was so certain. He'd suspected going in that that was the case. It was a relief to have it confirmed. The last thing he needed was to push an uncertain old man down an unknown path.

Now Slocum had to decide what *he* wanted to do. Should he keep his promise to Portia? Had he already kept it?

But he hadn't. And he knew it.

14

Slocum sat at a table in the corner. Pete Harney turned the bar over to his backup and brought two beers over. He took a long sip on his, then slid the other across the damp tabletop to Slocum.

"You're looking a whole lot better than the last time I saw you, Slocum."

"I hope so."

"Sheriff still don't have a lead on that killing, does he?"

"Not as far as I know."

"I been keeping my ears open, and I got a few bits and pieces might interest you. Come on in back." Harney took another sip, then stood up. He resettled the belt around his potbelly, and nodded toward the back room. Without waiting for Slocum, he moved away.

Slocum took a pull on his own beer, wiped his lips, and followed, leaving the beer at the table. The back room smelled of stale booze and damp sawdust. It was packed with crates and cases, bottles of every shape and size. A couple of rungless ladder-back chairs leaned against the wall. Harney grabbed one, spun it on one leg, and gave it a twist toward Slocum. He jerked the other away from the wall and sat down, leaning back against a stack of packing crates.

"You run a place like this, you hear just about everything sooner or later, John," he said. "Course, I'm supposed to be discreet, don't you know. Fella comes in, gets oiled up, he's gonna let something slip now and then. He likes to feel it ain't going no further."

Slocum listened quietly. He studied the big man, wondering how much was bluster and how much was a genuine crisis of conscience. That it was both was clear.

"What have you heard?"

"I got to have your word you won't tell a living soul you heard it from me."

Slocum nodded.

"Unh unh, John, shaking your damn head ain't gonna do it. Your *word,* I gotta have your word."

"You got it."

"Alright, now, see, it's only bits, like I said, but I don't know, I think there's something there. Smoke and fire, that sort of thing."

"If you don't spit it out, I'll die of old age before you get around to telling me."

"I know, I know. It's just . . . aw, hell, Johnny. I feel like I'm peachin' on a schoolmate, you know? It ain't easy. I know I talk a lot, but I don't usually say anything. This is kind of different for me."

Slocum decided to say nothing. The silence, he knew, would get on Pete's nerves, and he would talk just to break the uncomfortable quiet. Harney took another sip of the beer, ignoring the foam strip it left on his upper lip.

"Here goes nothing." Harney finished his beer. "Mackay was in yesterday. He was getting pretty drunk, as usual. He was talking to a couple of them boys he runs with, from the Broken Rail, Mitchell's spread."

"I know where he works, Pete. I just don't know when."

Harney laughed. "Me neither. Don't know why Mitchell puts up with it, tell you the truth. Anyhow, he was running his mouth about the big splash he was gonna make tonight. At the show. Said he was gonna be a star."

"And you think he's going to try something at the opening performance, is that it?"

"Part, yeah, part of it. But there's more. I don't know if there's a connection or not. Said he was 'studying acting,' I swear that's how he put it, 'studying acting' with one of them girls, Ramsey's girls. They was all laughing, and you and I both know he wasn't talkin' about no acting lessons. Don't surprise me none, them theater people being kind of loose and all."

Slocum was getting interested. "He say which?"

"Which what?"

"Which of Ramsey's girls was giving him the 'lessons'?"

"A redhead, he said. Said she was a real redhead, too. Said he learned that his first lesson."

Slocum sat back on the chair. He felt the wheels turning in his own head. So far, they weren't generating anything but noise. But he was getting a picture he didn't much care for.

"Anything else?"

"Now this I ain't sure about. I don't even know if I oughta say nothing."

"In for a penny, Pete . . . "

"What?"

"In for a penny, in for a pound."

"Oh, yeah. I know what you mean. Yeah, I suppose you're right. Well, he leaned close, you know, and I had to strain my ears some to catch this part. Even grabbed a rag to clean off a table so I could get closer. Said he done her a favor. Said something about putting the squeeze on one of them fancy boys."

"He say when?"

"Nope, why?"

"Well, there's only one now, so it must have been before Moseley got shot."

"Oh, now, Slocum, you don't think he meant . . . "

Slocum remembered the whispered conversation he'd overheard in a drugged haze. He wished he could identify the voices, but wishes didn't get it done. "I don't know what he meant, Pete. You tell the sheriff?"

"You crazy? Tell him what? Tell him Mackay was talkin' some foolishness after a few drinks? That's not news. Sheriff would lock me up for a fool, I tell him that. 'Sides, Ray Castle and Tommy Mitchell is old friends. One of his boys gets in trouble, Mitchell just pays a visit and things get fixed up, nice as you please."

"Even murder?"

"Now, you don't know that. I didn't say that, neither. What I'm sayin' is you need a lot more evidence to get Mackay than I got to give you. Ray Castle would want even more still. I don't know, maybe I should have kept my mouth shut."

"You did the right thing, Pete. Don't worry about it. I won't say anything."

"Guess you got to go to the show tonight, though, huh?"

"Guess I do."

Slocum sighed. He stood and walked to the back door. "This open, Pete?"

"Give it a push. Sometimes it sticks."

Slocum shoved the door open, ignoring the squeal of wood on wood, and stepped out into the alleyway. He looked up the block toward the rear of the hotel. He tried to remember how long ago it was that Pete had found him, sprawled on the old lumber pile, beaten nearly to a pulp. It was only a few days, but it seemed like forever.

He felt betrayed by Portia. There had been no promises.

It was strictly tit for tat, but he realized he had allowed
it to become something a little more than that. And now,
to learn that she might have conducted the same sort of
business, presumably with the same currency, with Brett
Mackay . . . Juliet Ramsey had red hair too, darker, but
still red. Maybe . . .

Harney stood in the doorway. "You alright, John? You
look kind of broke down."

Slocum shook his head. "I'm fine, Pete. Just thinking,
that's all."

"You think I ought to tell the sheriff about tonight, about
Mackay's plans?"

"Nope. Better let it happen, let me handle it. No sense
just putting a lid on it. It'll find some other way to blow.
The sooner the better, I think."

"I hope you know what you're doing. I'm starting to think
Mackay isn't quite the harmless bully I always reckoned."

"I guess we all learned something the past couple of days,
Pete. Question is, what do we do with it?"

He turned to look at Harney. The big bartender stroked
his chin. "You got me, John."

"I got to go."

Slocum stepped past him and into the back room. Without
a backward look, he pushed into the barroom, stopped at his
table to down the rest of his beer. He was halfway to the
front door when Harney caught up with him.

"John, you ain't going to do something stupid, are you?"

"Already have, Pete. I already have."

Outside, he debated whether to write off the whole thing,
turn his back on the professor and his scheming brood, ride
back to the Double Rocker, and get back to his normal life.
It was tempting, but it didn't sit right with him. He knew
himself well enough to know he was angry at having been
fooled, used. Following his dick around like a lovesick
schoolboy, he had walked into a stone wall. It could have
been worse. Portia wasn't guilty yet. Not for certain. He
knew that. But it didn't take any of the sting out of it.

His other choice, to confront Portia with the charge of treachery, seemed pointless. It would make him feel better for a few minutes, but the pain would still be there when the thrill of the confrontation was long gone. And if she denied it, what would he know that he didn't already know?

What did he owe her, what did he owe any of them, anyway? The answer was nothing, or it should have been. But Portia had been right about one thing. He'd taken an interest in Ramsey, pulled him out of the fire. He couldn't walk away now. Besides, the old man wasn't responsible for his daughters' tricks. It would be unfair to blame him, to leave him to Mackay.

Shaking his head as if he'd just solved the mystery of life, Slocum headed back to Ramsey's tent. The sun was starting to climb into the sky, filling it with a white haze. The tent itself looked deserted when he got there. He pushed inside, conscious of the glow, light filtering through the canvas, highlighting the red stripes against the sky. A lone figure sat on the stage, now fully dressed for the evening performance.

Whoever it was didn't seem to notice him. Surpressing the urge to shout, he walked quietly toward the low platform. The closer he got, the more imposing the backdrop became. Tall flats, their paint splashed in bold swatches, depicted some sort of stone walls. High windows marked two of them. It looked like a castle of some sort.

The figure on the stage, her back to him, sat motionless. Her shoulders were hunched, her head covered in a hood of some sort, a dark gray, almost like a nun's habit. He stepped onto the stage. The woman started, but didn't look around.

"I suppose you have stage fright," he said.

The woman shook her head. He stepped around to face her, expecting Portia. But he was wrong. Cordelia sat there, her hands in her lap, clasped almost as if in prayer.

She glanced at him without expression. "What do you want?"

"I, actually, I was looking for your sister."

"Which one?"

"Portia . . . she around?"

"Oh yes, she's around. She's always around . . . when she's not sleeping around." Slocum was not prepared for the bitterness. "I suppose it's your turn, is it?"

"My turn? What do you mean?"

"I would have thought she'd have gotten to you sooner. You're less loathsome than some of her bedmates. Not all, but some."

"Look, I—"

"No, you look, Mr. Slocum. You helped my father. I appreciate it. He appreciates it. But you don't belong here. You're not part of this family. Its business doesn't concern you."

"What are you talking about?"

"You know damn well what I'm talking about. You tried to talk my father into giving up the troupe. You didn't do that on your own. I know that. It must have been Portia, or Juliet. But it doesn't concern you. You should just mind your own business. Please leave."

"But—"

"No, no buts, Mr. Slocum. Portia did what she did, and you did what she wanted you to do. That's as far as it goes. You owe her nothing. She can't be that good in bed. Just let it be."

"But—"

"*Please,* Mr. Slocum. Let it be."

"Is Portia here?"

"No. She and her husband have gone for a ride."

"Her husband?"

"Oh, you mean to say she didn't tell you? Have I been underestimating you, Mr. Slocum? Would it have made a difference if you had known? Don't bother to answer that. I'll pay you the compliment of believing that it might have."

"Look, Cordelia, I don't know what you think I'm doing here, but—"

"No, you look, Mr. Slocum. I know *exactly* what you're doing here. Dogs are all alike. They come around sniffing after a bitch in heat. Since that is almost always fair Portia, it follows that you are here to see her. Since this particular bitch gives away nothing without a price, it also follows that you meddled in our affairs in exchange for her sexual favors. Good day, Mr. Slocum."

"Cordelia, I—"

"Good *day*, Mr. Slocum."

She sprang to her feet and dashed off the stage.

15

Slocum was one of the first to arrive. He took a seat in the middle of the big tent, sliding to the far end of the last row and putting his hat under the makeshift bench. More than half of the audience would have to stand, and the seats were less than comfortable in any case.

He'd been to the theater a few times, but he was used to the formality attendant upon such occasions. St. Louis and New Orleans had well-established theaters, large, permanent buildings sporting the latest and most excessive ornamentation. Even Denver fancied itself cultured. But an itinerant company like Ramsey's couldn't afford to worry about gold leaf and plaster friezes. They needed something to keep the weather off, and that's pretty much where the amenities stopped.

As he sat there, people began to file in, family groups wearing their Sunday best, farmers who hadn't bothered to change, or who had nothing much to change into. Even a few cowboys, wearing clean shirts and a quart of hair oil under sweat-stained Stetsons, had filtered in.

Scraps of conversation reached him, then were swept away by flurries of activity as more people filed in. The seats were at a premium, and Ramsey, conscious of public relations, had reserved a few of the choicest benches for the leading citizens of Dry Spring. Some of the more prosperous ranchers, wearing wives on their arms the way they usually wore guns on their hips, waved to one another as they took their seats up front.

"Ready for a great show?" Startled, Slocum turned to see who had spoken and found a grinning Paddy Gibson planted behind him. "Didn't know you was the cultured type, Slocum."

"What the hell are *you* doing here?"

"Hell, man, I'm part of the show."

"You?"

"Every show needs somethin' to keep folks occupied until it gets goin', and durin' the intermission, too. I'll be doin' my best to do just that."

"Doing what?"

Gibson nodded. "See that there piano? Who you think is gonna tickle them keys? Yours truly, that's who. And don't say nothin'. I done it before. Didn't always make a living pouring slop down cowboys' ugly pusses." He wiggled his fingers ostentatiously. "All them lessons back in Pennsylvania gonna come in right handy. Make myself a nice piece of change, too."

"Maybe I ought to think about this."

"Now, come on, Slocum. You heard me over to Harney's. I ain't bad. Not that most people here'd know the difference. Maybe Missus Mitchell would. But that's different. She's English, after all. Heard lots better'n me. But she's about the only one I got to worry about."

"Good luck, Paddy."

"You too."

"I don't need it."

"The hell you don't. Mackay don't get you, I think one a them little Ramsey girls will. That little one was cussin' a blue streak this morning. I bet your ears was burnin' all afternoon. I know mine was."

"What are you talking about, Paddy?"

"Gotta go, Johnny. Maybe I'll see you after the show. Have a drink down at Harney's."

Slocum watched Gibson thread his way through the thickening crowd in the center aisle, then climb onto the stage and take a seat at an upright piano. So far, there was no sign of Brett Mackay. Slocum didn't know whether that was good or bad. If the cowboy were in the crowd, at least he could keep an eye on him. If he had something else in mind, it might be a little tougher to ride herd on him.

Strains of Stephen Foster started to curl above the buzz of the crowd as Gibson tried to compete with animated conversation. Slocum stood and stretched, scanning the back of the tent without calling attention to himself.

People had begun to settle down as Slocum checked his watch. It was seven-thirty, fifteen minutes until curtain. Ramsey strode onto the stage accompanied by a fanfare from Paddy's piano. The crowd hushed as Ramsey stepped to the front of the stage. He looked imposing in his costume, a gleaming breastplate bulking him up a little, concealing the more fragile frame on which it hung.

"Good evening, ladies and gentlemen," he said, raising both hands for quiet. "Welcome to our theater. I am sorry it couldn't be more imposing, but then, as Shakespeare said, 'The play's the thing,' and I believe he was correct. As you know, this evening's program will feature *Macbeth*, with yours truly in the title role. It is a piece I have done scores of times, and witnessed scores more. My work has been compared not unfavorably with that of Edwin Forrest and even the immortal Edwin Booth. For your added pleasure, Mr. Patrick Gibson will provide a program of piano favorites until curtain, and also during the intermission. I'd like to ask your cooperation in a few small matters. If the gentlemen would refrain from smoking, particularly cigars, in deference to the ladies in attendance, it would be much appreciated. We'd also like you to keep to your seats, those of you who have them, during the play. And those of you standing in the rear, if you would try not to jostle your neighbors, and make sure everyone has enough space for comfortable standing, we'll all enjoy the program that much more."

Ramsey paused a moment, his eyes sweeping the audience, a stern look on his face. It grew quiet, and he continued. "On behalf of myself and the entire company, I'd like to thank you for your patronage, and to remind you that we will be doing *Macbeth* again tomorrow and the night after. Then, on Friday, Saturday, and Sunday, we'll be presenting one of my personal favorites, a play I had the privilege to perform in New York, under the direction of its author, *The Octoroon* by Dion Boucicault. Again, I thank you."

The professor bowed dramatically, sweeping the floorboards with his right hand. To a smattering of polite applause, he stepped back from the stage and into the wings.

Gibson cranked up the piano, pounding the keys a little harder, to be heard above the steady din. The makeshift lights dimmed, as one of the crew tilted a cover up and over the row of oil lamps serving as footlights.

Paddy finished with a flourish, and a hush fell over the audience as three shadowy figures materialized at center stage. Slocum, like the others present, took his seat. He leaned forward, curious in spite of himself. The shield was tilted back, and an orange glow flooded the front edge of the stage.

The three figures were thrown into sharp relief, and Slocum inhaled sharply as he realized all of Ramsey's daughters, made up as three witches, were on stage before him. He was so caught up in watching the women, the words went right past him. The lights dimmed again before he could identify who was who. He borrowed a printed program from the man seated beside him just to verify what he thought he had seen.

As the lights came up again, a commotion broke out in the rear of the tent, and Slocum turned in his seat. Over the craning heads behind him, and the crowd standing behind the last row of seats, it was all but impossible to see what was happening. He got to his feet, barely conscious of the play going on behind him. Four or five men were pushing and shoving in the mouth of the tent, and Slocum slipped along the side of the canvas, skirting the last seats and easing through the edge of the crowd.

As he neared the entrance, he spotted Brett Mackay and some of his cronies. Mackay had the young man who was taking tickets by the front of his shirt. The kid's feet were just about off the floor as Mackay shook him roughly, then gave him a shove. The kid tried to keep his balance, but his feet went out from under him and he landed heavily on his back.

Slocum pushed through the last few onlookers and grabbed Mackay by the back of the shirt. The big cowboy turned angrily. He had been drinking, and his sagging features looked slightly out of kilter. He jerked free of Slocum's grip, lost his balance, and staggered back two or three steps before regaining his equilibrium.

"What the hell do you want, Slocum? Haven't you left town yet?"

"Does it look like it, Mackay?"

The cowboy lunged, and Slocum sidestepped, sticking out a foot. Mackay, his reactions dulled by liquor, saw the foot but was unable to stop his charge. He tripped and went down heavily on his stomach, knocking the air from his lungs. Slocum landed on him with one knee planted in the middle of his back.

"Hey," one of Mackay's allies shouted, taking a step forward.

Slocum unholstered the Colt and waved it. "Back off, gents."

"You're a dead man, Slocum," Mackay shouted. Slocum ignored him, grinding his knee into the small of the cowboy's back and shoving his face into the ground. Mackay continued to squirm and curse, but the words were muffled by the pressure. His friends started to close on Slocum, but froze as Slocum cocked the Colt and stuck it behind Mackay's right ear.

"Unless you want to see daylight through this man's head come sunup, I think you boys ought to calm down, take this sonofabitch in hand, and get him sobered up."

"You bastard," one of them shouted.

Slocum started to get up, and the shouter shrank back a couple of steps. "Think you're tough, don't you, sticking that damn gun in a man's ear. You didn't have it, I'd show you something."

"You were smart, you'd show me your tails, right now."

"Go to hell."

Slocum was on his feet now. "Have it your way," he said. He was vaguely aware of someone pulling at his arm. He turned with the pistol ready, and narrowly missed lashing Cordelia across the face with the barrel.

"Please, just make them leave. No shooting, please. No violence. It isn't necessary. Just make them leave."

Slocum thought about arguing, but he didn't really want violence any more than Cordelia did. He turned away from her. "You heard the lady, gents, just go on home, and nobody has to get hurt."

"No ladies here, Slocum," Mackay grinned. "You ought to know that. I heard all about this little witch's midnight visit to you. I reckon most people in town have."

Slocum lashed out with the Colt, catching Mackay on the side of the head. The big man tried to duck, but the barrel of the revolver glanced off his temple. Cushioned by his hat, the blow knocked his hat off but did no real damage. Mackay teetered, raising his hands to signal his retreat. "Alright, alright," he said. "I'm goin'."

He staggered backward out of the tent, his cronies backing out after him. When they were gone, Slocum turned to Cordelia. "I'm sorry about that," he said.

But Cordelia said nothing. Giving him a glance as full of scorn as any he'd ever seen, she turned and disappeared into the crowd. He stood there quietly, watched her step onto the stage, then made his way back to his seat.

In the best show business fashion, Ramsey took up in mid line as if nothing had happened. Slocum sat slumped in his seat, barely paying attention to the play. He had learned something, at least. Pete Harney had not been imagining the threat to the performance. If that was accurate, he wondered, what else was?

At intermission, Slocum was hopelessly lost, not just in the play, but in the situation. The crowd milled around, some moving closer to the stage to listen to Gibson's piano, while others stepped outside for a smoke and a breath of fresh air. Slocum stayed in his seat. He wanted to leave but seemed incapable of making a decision one way or the other. As much as he wanted to disappear, part of him also realized that as long as the performance continued, there was a chance that Mackay might return. He was probably sitting in one of the saloons, stoking up on liquid courage, planning his return to center stage.

When the play resumed, Slocum paid only sporadic attention. He watched closely only when Portia, who was playing to type as Lady Macbeth, egged her husband on. He kept losing the thread of the play, reading personal details into the situations. The truth was, he didn't give a damn about Shakespeare at the moment, and wished the Ramseys, father and daughters, well gone. Punching cows was all he wanted.

When the first gunshot cracked in the rear of the tent, he didn't realize it wasn't part of the play. When the people around him started to shout, he turned but could see nothing. A woman screamed, and people started to rush toward the exit. A small knot of men charged toward the stage, bucking the tide. Ramsey, out of character for the first time, stood at the edge of the stage flailing his arms.

"This is an outrage, I say, an outrage. What is the meaning of this?" His voice carried over the steady droning of the crowd. Shouts punctuated his address as the knot of men bore down on the stage. Ramsey, confused and frightened, drew his prop sword and waved it at the charging band.

It didn't take a genius to realize the men weren't enraged critics. Hands sprouted like barren tree limbs from the charging men and Ramsey was hauled bodily from the stage and disappeared. Slocum tried to fight his way forward, but the pressing throng carried him backward a step for every one he took. Finally, drawing his own gun, he fired into the air, parting the mob in front of him and leaping over benches on his way toward the stage.

He charged into the milling band, flailing with his pistol. He fired twice more, but it was already too late. He caught a fist in mid flight and wrenched it back, snapping an arm at the elbow, then tossing the moaning cowboy to one side. Somewhere at the bottom of the pile, Clayton Ramsey screamed for help. Slocum fired once more then stuck his revolver into a man's ear.

"Call them off, you bastard. Now!"

The man stared at him dumbly, and Slocum lashed him across the face with his pistol, opening a gash in the man's cheek. He dragged another man free and finally got his hands on Brett Mackay. Closing his hands around Mackay's throat, he dragged him backward, tripping over a fallen bench and landing heavily, Mackay on top of him. His tender ribs threatened to cave in, but Mackay was too drunk to exploit his advantage. Slocum wriggled free, getting to his feet in time to drive a booted foot into Mackay's throat. The cowboy collapsed like a poleaxed steer, vomited, and lay there writhing in his own puke.

"Get up, you bastard. Get the fuck up!"

Mackay continued to groan, his hands closed over his throat. Slocum kicked him again and again, driving his boot into Mackay's ribs. "You sonofabitch, I'll fucking kill you. I'll kill you, you bastard."

Hands grabbed him from behind, and he shook them off. He threw himself forward, straddling Mackay and driving his fist into the unguarded face. He felt the squash of cartilage as he caved in the cowboy's nose, the warm splash of blood on his knuckles as he hit him again.

Again hands closed on him from behind, and he was conscious for the first time of screaming. He fell backward, and Mackay tried to crawl away. The men with him grabbed Mackay by the arms and tried to pull him free, but Slocum wouldn't let go. He held on with both hands, twisting Mackay's leg until it slipped from his grasp.

"That's all, that's all, please stop it. No more." He looked up and realized it was Cordelia. He lay there gasping for breath, stunned by his own rage, the ferocity of his assault. His tongue felt like a leather strap, his throat burned, and he realized he had been shouting at the top of his lungs. Cordelia, staring at him as if he were a mad dog, backed away as he reached out a hand. She buried her face in her hands and ran. Mackay disappeared through the open exit, and Slocum sat there, cradling Ramsey's battered head in his arms. The old man was in a bad way. His face was already swollen, and blood seeped from one corner of his mouth and gushed from his nose.

"It's alright, Professor," he said, again and again, as if wishing would make it so. "It's alright, Professor."

He felt the old man's hand close on his wrist. The look in the old actor's one open eye was one of confusion and despair. It wasn't alright, and only this beaten old man seemed to know it.

16

Slocum walked past the Pinon Saloon. He wanted a drink, but he knew there'd be no stopping at one. In the back of his mind was the thought that Mackay might be there and he could finish it. But that wasn't a good idea either. He needed time to think, to put everything in perspective. He had a decision to make, and he knew it was one of those decisions there'd be no undoing. It had better be right.

He pushed into the hotel lobby half expecting a lynch party of some of Mackay's friends, but only the clerk stared back at him as he stood in the doorway.

The clerk nodded, and Slocum stalked past him. Taking the stairs two at a time, he made the landing and rushed down the corridor to his room like a kid running from an animal in a dream. He slammed the door, locked it, and

116

struck a match. He found the lamp and realized as he tried
to light it that his hands were trembling. Still full of rage,
he smashed a fist into the wall, bruising his knuckles. The
match burned his fingers, and he cursed softly. Striking a
second match, he got the lamp lit, replaced the chimney
with a clatter, and took a deep breath.

Sitting on the bed, he pulled the Colt. He held it for a
long time, just looking at it as if it were something he'd
found in the street. Then, with mechanical movements, he
opened the cylinder and popped the empty shells onto the
floor. Reloading the gun, he placed it on the bed beside
him. Every once in a while he reached out blindly to feel
the cold metal, as if to reassure himself it was still there.

What he should do, he knew, was get the hell out. The
best thing for everyone would be if he put as much distance
between himself and Dry Spring as possible. The sooner the
better. That would be best.

But he couldn't.

He knew he couldn't, but he wasn't sure why. It wasn't
that he cared what they might think of him, Gibson, Harney,
and the others. They could think him a coward or a madman,
it was all the same to him. But something about this business
left him feeling empty. There was a hollowness deep in
his gut, one that leaving would just expand until he burst
like a balloon with too much air in it. What he needed,
for peace of mind, and to fill that emptiness, was to
put a period to Dry Spring. And Brett Mackay. It was
Mackay, that was the unfinished business. All the rest of it
was meaningless. Portia, Cordelia, Ramsey himself, Juliet.
They were bit players. But Mackay was different. Slocum
no longer doubted it was Mackay who had blindsided him
and left him in the alley. He no longer doubted, either, that
it was Mackay who had killed Moseley.

There was something eating at Mackay, some homicidal
passion. You could see it in his eyes. And when he drank,
which he seemed to be doing more and more often, whatever
it was swam closer to the surface. It lurked just under the

pink mist, some viper, peering up through the haze, waiting for someone to come close enough to strike. Whatever it was had killed Moseley, whatever it was had almost killed Ramsey. And, worst of all, whatever it was had spoken directly to something of the same species in Slocum himself. Kill Mackay, and it died. It was impossible to invent a more primal algebra.

But Slocum didn't know what to do about any of that. He didn't know what to do about anything, at this point. He lay back, his hand resting on the Colt, and stared at the door as if expecting it to open of its own accord. His eyes closed, and he felt himself drifting again. It was like using the laudanum; he was detached, floating in midair, spinning. He thought he could look at himself from a great height. He examined himself lying there, as if he were staring at his own image in a mirror at a great distance.

Slocum didn't like what he saw.

Engrossed in the dreamlike fog, he didn't hear the first knock on the door. The second seemed part of the dream, an unseen drum beaten by an invisible hand. He shook himself and got to his feet on the third knock, nearly falling as he started toward the door. He ran back for the Colt and cocked it, muffling the sound with his left hand.

Undoing the latch, he held the Colt pointed at the ceiling. With the latch off, he yelled, "Come in."

The door opened slowly, a frail hand on the knob.

"Slocum?"

It was Portia. She stepped in, her face still smeared with traces of makeup, thick dark lines painted to give her the wizened face of Lady Macbeth. "Slocum," she said again, stepping across the threshold. He backed away, lowering the pistol. She stared at him, watching the gun as he dropped it into his holster.

"What are you doing here?" he asked.

"I . . . I have to talk to you. I didn't know where else to go, who to talk to."

"Well, you still don't."

"Slocum, you can't turn your back on me. Not now. Not after . . . "

"After what? After making love to you? Is that what you were going to say? Well, I got news for you, lady, that wasn't making love, that was just a good poke. The kind you usually have to pay two dollars for."

He thought she was going to smack him, and braced for the assault, but her hand just hovered in the air, then fumbled with her hair, pressing stiff, stray, artificially gray strands close to her temple. She looked bewildered.

"No," she said. "No. That isn't what I was going to say."

"Well, spit it out, Portia. I don't have all night."

"I need your help. I . . . I've done something terrible, and I don't know what . . . how to . . . "

She shook her head, then stared at him helplessly. Her eyes grew large, and tears began to well up. They trickled down her cheeks, smearing the makeup still further, etching serpentine lines as they dribbled to her chin then dripped on her blouse. She took a tentative step toward him, but he held up a hand.

She recoiled as if he'd slapped her. Her hands reached out for him, but he backed away. "No."

"But . . . "

"No, damn it, Portia. Just no. If you have something to say, say it. If not, I have things to do."

She turned away and reached for the door. He thought she was going to pull it closed behind her, but she just leaned her head against its edge. Her shoulders shook, but the crying made not a sound. He hated himself for being so cold, but she had it coming, and they both knew it. Maybe this would restore some balance between them, make them somehow even.

Maybe.

"How's the professor?" It sounded colder than he meant it. "I mean, is he alright?"

"He'll live, if that's what you mean."

"No, that's not what I meant. I want to know how he is. He took quite a beating."

"That's my fault," she said.

"Yes, I suppose it is, partly. But there's nothing you can do about it now. It's happened, and you'll have to live with it. Maybe you can learn something from it."

She whirled on him. "Why are you so damned hostile? What did I ever do to you?"

"Why don't you ask your husband that question? I'll bet he'd have an answer."

She staggered then, and he thought she might fall. "Oh, I see."

"Yes. I do too. Now."

"Slocum, I don't blame you for thinking that I was just . . . " She seemed at a loss for words. Her head swiveled from side to side, but no words came.

"Using me? Is that what you were looking for?"

She nodded. "Yes. But it wasn't that way. I swear to you. It wasn't. When I came here, I thought maybe . . . but what happened, that was real. I wasn't going to do it. But it happened. Not because I planned it. Not because I thought I could get something I wanted. It happened because I wanted it to." She looked him straight in the eye for the first time. "And you did to."

He said nothing.

"Didn't you?"

He closed the door.

"Didn't you? Answer me, damn it. You wanted it too, didn't you?"

"It doesn't matter what I wanted. Not now."

"Yes it does. You're hurt, and I'm sorry for that. But—"

"You're sorry for a lot of things these days, aren't you, Portia? You've made a general mess of things, not just of your life, but of your father's, your sisters' lives—"

"And yours, right. That's what you're angry about."

"No. That's not what I'm angry about. I'm angry about thinking you were somebody you're not. I'm angry because

I was stupid, not because you were manipulative. I feel stupid. But it doesn't hurt. Not really. I've learned something useful."

"But that doesn't change anything. Not really. My father needs help, and so do the rest of us."

"I can't help. I don't even know if I would help if I could. I'm sorry."

"But you don't even know why. You don't understand."

"I don't have to understand to know what I feel. And that's what matters."

"Would it help any if I told you my husband has left me? Would that make a difference?"

"No, it wouldn't. Even if I were dumb enough to believe it. Right now, I think you'd say just about anything. You're drowning, and you need somebody to haul you out. But I'm fresh out of rope, Portia. I can't help. I'm leaving in the morning."

"But you can't leave."

"Watch me."

"You don't understand. Raymond did leave me. This morning. And something terrible is going to happen. I can feel it."

"Oh really? I held your father's bloody head in my lap tonight. That's about as terrible as anything I want to see."

"That's what I'm talking about."

"I know. And I know more than that. I know you bought Mackay for fifty dollars and a roll in the hay."

"No!"

"I heard you. I know what I heard. It's all fitting into place now. I *heard* you, Portia. Don't you understand? You bought him, but you got more than you bargained for. I don't know, maybe you gave him more than he was used to, and he thinks he owes it to you. The joke's on him, huh?"

"You're hateful, Slocum. You're a terrible, hateful man."

"We already know what you are, don't we, girl?"

This time, she did smack him. It was a crushing blow.

She swung from the heels, then rounded to swing at him again. She darted forward, and he sidestepped. She lost her balance and stumbled just as the door swung open.

Cordelia stood in the doorway, her face frozen in amazement. "Even now, you act like this. For God's sake, Portia, don't you have any self-respect at all?"

Portia backed away from Slocum, turning toward her sister. "It . . . it's not what it looks like, Cory. I—"

"No, I suppose it isn't. But then, it never is, with you, is it? You're just an innocent little girl. You don't know how these things happen. Your clothes take themselves off, some strange ghost spreads your legs. Your hips move all by themselves. It's a goddamn mystery! Isn't it? Damn you—"

"She's telling the truth, Miss Ramsey," Slocum said.

"Oh, and I suppose you're a paragon of integrity? I can trust you implicitly, can't I, Mr. Slocum? But then, you've already had her. You don't need to lie. Do you? Do you, dammit?"

She turned and ran down the hall. Portia raced after her. Slocum stood in the doorway, thoroughly confused and more uncertain than ever.

He was still standing there ten minutes later, when Portia returned. "She wouldn't listen to me," she said. "But somebody has to. Somebody has to hear what I have to say."

Slocum nodded. "Alright. I'll listen."

Her head jerked up. She peered at him through a fog of old tears, leaning close, as if she expected him to break out laughing at her expense.

He took her hand and pulled her into the room. Kicking the door closed, he steered her toward a chair. She sat mindlessly and stared up into his face.

"Please, let me finish before you say anything."

"Why not?" he asked. "Why not?"

17

Ray Castle nodded to Slocum without looking up from his desk. "Slocum, what's on your mind?"

"Well, Sheriff, you asked me to drop around. I'm dropping."

"That all?"

"Nope. I thought I might ride out to that creek where I found Moseley, take a look around. Unless you have any objection."

"Not as long as you don't go no further. I don't guess I'm ever going to get to the bottom of that Moseley killing. But you never know."

"Fine. You know where I'll be."

"Unh huh. And if you ain't, you know I'll find you anyhow. Don't you?"

"If you say so."

"Oh, I do, Slocum. I do say so."

Slocum didn't bother to say goodbye. He stepped into the hot sun and took a long look at Dry Spring. It looked like a hundred other cow towns he'd been in. And if he left now, he wouldn't miss it, that was for sure. It looked to him now the way a hangover headache felt. No reason to miss that.

He swung into the saddle a little stiffly. Still aching a little from the beating, the encounter with Mackay the night before hadn't helped any. But he was serviceable. He could give a day's work for a day's wage. That was good enough.

He rode straight out of town without looking to either side. From the corner of his eye, he thought he saw Pete Harney in the window of his saloon, but he didn't turn to make sure. No reason to. Harney had been a friend, and that counted for something. But Pete would want to know what he was up to. Since he wasn't sure of the answer, he didn't want anyone, not even a friend, to ask.

Again, he wondered whether he would stop at the creek or just keep on riding. He was wanted in half a dozen places he knew of, maybe as many more he didn't know about. Pete was a friend, so was Paddy Gibson. But he'd made a career of leaving friends behind. It was easier not to say goodbye. And even thinking about it made him waver. He was already too confused. Tugging a few heartstrings would only make it worse. If he came back, fine. And if he didn't, well . . .

Slocum rode past the theater tent, and the little wagon train that had brought it to such grief. Glancing once, he saw no one, and didn't bother to look back. He could almost feel it falling away behind him. Conscious of it, the way you're conscious of a pair of hidden eyes stabbing you between the shoulder blades, he didn't dare look back.

Out on the flat, he looked uphill all the way, at the sky as far west as he could see, where a few clouds seemed to perch on the purple mountains. It was tempting to light out for them, see if maybe he couldn't touch them after all. But a deal is a deal, and he had made a deal with Portia. Maybe it was a devil's bargain, but he'd made a few of those in his time, too. And he still owed the Double Rocker three more months. He'd shaken Tim Baker's hand on that, and he would deliver the time. But that was all.

At the top of the first rise, he was tempted to look back, just once. But there was no reason. Or there were too many reasons. He thought about his obligation to Clayton Ramsey. Was it really an obligation, or had he talked himself into it? Or, worse still, had Portia seduced him into assuming it?

Either way, was it real?

As he headed downhill, he tried to shrug off the guilt, reasoning it shouldn't be hard unless it was real. But he could even deal with that, when and if he could decide.

At the next ridge, he looked down on the stand of cottonwoods where he'd found Moseley's body. It seemed almost as if he were going through it all again, for some reason he didn't understand. He angled away to the south, planning on giving the trees a wide berth. As his horse kneed into the creek, he glanced upstream. Nothing but light and moving leaves. The place was as desolate as it had been. There was nothing there to see, or was there?

Louis Marillac was missing. But it seemed unlikely he'd be found in the same place, alive or dead. Ramsey didn't even think the dwarf was anything to worry about. He'd said Louis ran off from time to time, when someone hurt his feelings. Cordelia didn't agree, but then she seldom agreed with anyone about anything. Portia just didn't know, or claimed not to. It was all the same.

But he said he'd see it through, and he would. Even if it meant stumbling around in circles. But sometimes, there was no point in chewing cabbage twice. His grandmother had told him that a long time ago. He hadn't understood what she meant then, and he wasn't sure he did yet. But he was starting to.

Castle had come out here to look around. The sheriff
had found nothing. That was all there was to it. Or should
be. But was Castle really looking? Or did he even give a
damn some kid had been backshot and left to die? Did
anybody?

That, too, was an imponderable. But it wasn't somebody
else's problem, it was his, Ray Castle and all his good
intentions aside. Slocum leaned into the rise as his horse
climbed out of the creek on the far bank, then shouldered its
way through the tall grass. He tugged on the reins, nudging
the horse back toward the trail. Now that he was on the far
side, there was no reason to be wary of the scene. It was
past seducing him.

He found the trail a few minutes later. Goaded by some
unexplained chill, he dug his spurs into the chestnut's flanks.
The horse seemed reluctant to respond, shaking its head and
moving only grudgingly faster. He dug the spurs in again,
and the horse spurted forward, pushing itself now, as the
trail sloped sharply upward. At the ridgeline, he stopped
again. This time he stood in the stirrups and looked back
toward the valley floor.

On the near side of the trees, just above the waterline,
he saw a flash of light. He waited patiently, but it wasn't
repeated. It could have been nothing, a sudden ripple, maybe
a fish jumping and the splash catching the sun. He waited a
couple of minutes, then shrugged it away. It was just one
more little thing to forget about.

Heading downhill again, he tried to push it all out of his
mind. What he really needed was a few days away from
the place, a new perspective. If he could throw himself into
something, something to wear him out, it would be better
than the laudanum. He could sweat it all out, then sleep it
away. But that wasn't in the cards. Not yet, anyway.

He pushed the horse into a steady trot, not wanting to
tire it, but wishing he could pick up the interrupted strands
of his life. This time, the horse seemed agreeable, settling
into its stride almost effortlessly. He was getting thirsty,

and he tugged his canteen off the pommel. He slowed the horse to a walk and unscrewed the cap. The water tasted of metal. It was warm and a little bitter. He scraped at the accumulation of salts around the canteen mouth, careful not to knock them into the water. The second mouthful tasted a little better, but not much. He'd have to refill at the next stream, scrape the scaly white deposits away and rinse the canteen a couple of times.

The valley in front of him had no water, and he'd have to wait. He took a third mouthful, swirled it around, then spat it out. It would have to do. He screwed the cap back on, draped the leather strap over the pommel, and slapped at the horse with his reins. He wished he had a plan. But moving at least might let him clear his head, wipe away the cobwebs, and the scent of Portia.

Sitting there on the crest, he wondered what he was looking for. Brett Mackay was at the heart of the matter, but how? Portia's version was interesting, even credible, but he was through taking secondhand history for fact. He had to see for himself. He wanted to eyeball Mackay in that split second when there is no other witness but the Grim Reaper. That's when you saw the truth, plain, unvarnished, smooth as a baby's butt and clear as spring water. Look into a man's eyes at a moment like that, and he had no secrets from you. None.

The horse dove into the descent, and Slocum felt as if he were falling down a long flight of stairs. He had to saw at the bit to slow the chestnut. Something just wasn't right. It seemed almost as if he had stumbled somehow into another life. He had become someone who was out of tune. He did things without thinking, things that had always come naturally, and that he shouldn't have to think about. But he did them wrong, as if he had forgotten something, or never learned it at all.

He tried to shrug it off, thinking maybe it was a consequence of his injury, and the drug. But he wasn't taking the drug any longer, and his head shouldn't have been emptied of things as natural as breathing. It took him a while to understand it. And when he did, it was like a flash of lightning on a dark night: he *was* someone else, and someplace else. He was running away, and he didn't like it. It *didn't* come naturally to him.

At the valley floor, he angled to the right, taking his horse off the trail into the tall grass and scattered brush. He needed time to think. Too much had happened, and he had to sort it out before he did something he couldn't undo. He found a small clump of trees and reined in. He dropped to the ground and tethered his mount to a scrub pine.

Sitting down with his back against a boulder, for a long time he watched the clouds drifting toward him. Their shapes kept changing, and he was mesmerized by them. They grew darker, and a huge thunderhead spouted up in slow motion, its top flattening out like an anvil and smearing across the sky. The clouds boiled like floodwater, and they darkened almost by the moment.

Then he heard hoofbeats and got to his feet. Coming over the ridge, three men, riding hard, charged downhill. They were too distant for him to recognize them. He wondered why he hadn't heard them before. If they had been riding flat out, he should have seen them when he looked down the ridge behind him, but he hadn't. Or had he?

He remembered the bright flash at the creek. Maybe it hadn't been a fish after all. As they neared the bottom, they slowed. The lead rider, a few yards ahead of the others, reined in suddenly, holding up a hand to signal the two men behind him. He dropped from his horse and almost disappeared. Just his head and shoulders were visible above the tall grass. Slocum watched as the two mounted men nudged their horses closer. The man on foot seemed to be pointing something out. They shook their heads, then dismounted. A moment later, three hats started to move through the grass in single file.

Slocum realized they were following his path through the grass. About twenty yards in, they spread out, one man keeping to the path while the others moved fifteen or twenty yards to either side. They weren't just following, they were stalking. Slocum thought about hightailing it, but only for a moment. He was through running.

18

He moved quietly to his horse and jerked a Winchester carbine from its boot. He slipped his hand into a saddlebag and scooped a handful of shells from the box, tucked them into his pocket, and backed toward the trees. He could still see two of the hats, but the third one, the center man, had disappeared. Slocum backed through the trees, then cut on an angle through the sparse scrub until he hit the grass again.

Parting the grass carefully with his free hand, he tried to disguise his passage as much as possible, slipping sidewise and brushing the grass back in place as best he could. They could still track him, but there was no sense in making it easy for them. Three to one wasn't bad odds, as long as he had the advantage of movement. If they pinned him down, it would be a different story.

Sixty yards from the trees, he found a small clump of rocks. The grass thinned as it approached the boulders, then thickened again on the far side. It would be noticeable from above, but in the grass itself, he hadn't noticed it until he got within fifteen feet.

The boulders offered him about as much cover as he was going to get. He watched as the men signaled to one another with their hands. So far, they didn't realize he'd seen them. But once they found the horse, that would change.

As they drew closer, they slowed. Slocum could see them ducking, poking in the tall grass on either side. They reached the trees and he saw his horse shy away as one of the cowboys patted him on the rump. The men were talking softly, and he could see all three of them. It would be easy to drop one, maybe two, but he couldn't bring himself to do it. Confronting them had its own drawbacks, so he waited.

They fanned out, skirting the edge of the tree stand, looking for some indication of which way he'd gone. He recognized two of them now. Both of them were Mackay's buddies. The third man, who seemed to be the leader, he'd never seen before. He was also the tracker, and it was he who found Slocum's trail into the grass.

He waved the others after him. Again, they fanned out. They were close enough to hear now. Feet crunching crisp stalks of grass, snapping an occasional twig. Even the whisk of the grass on their legs as they tried to muffle their progress drifted to him on the hot breeze.

They were forming a rough semicircle now. The point man had begun to hang back a little, letting the wing men get out ahead of him. Slocum was dead center. If he let them get past him, he'd be alright, but if they surrounded him, whether by accident or not, he'd be in big trouble. Already, the man on the left had come almost even with him. The right wing was still a few yards short. The point man was twenty yards away, almost dead ahead.

He pressed himself down against the boulders, debating whether to bide his time or charge ahead full tilt. If he dropped the man in front of him, the grass would give him some cover, but he was in no shape for a prolonged race through the thick grass. And if he had to hit the ground, he might have trouble getting up.

He brought the Winchester up and made sure the safety was off. He leveled the sights, watching the point man drift from side to side as he poked in the grass with one boot. Partially blocked out by the metal sights, his face looked like a pink moon floating just above the tallest blades.

The right wing man was past him now, and Slocum was getting nervous. He couldn't afford to take his eyes off the point man. A heavy thud in the weeds to his left tugged at his attention, and he wanted to turn, but didn't dare. The left wing cursed, and Slocum heard the slap of flesh on denim as the man brushed burrs from his jeans.

The point man stopped suddenly. It looked as if he were staring straight at Slocum, and Slocum pulled the hammer back on the Winchester. Then the point man slid to the left a little. He seemed to be looking at something behind the rocks, partway up the slope behind Slocum.

Crouching down behind the rocks, Slocum tucked his head in tight against his shoulder and chewed on his tongue. He heard the man wade through the stiff-bladed saw grass, his boots crunching at the brittle roots, and then he was past. The crunching continued for a dozen steps, stopped, and Slocum held his breath until they resumed.

Slowly, Slocum raised his head. His legs cramped, and he stretched one out in front of him to relieve the stiffness. He could feel a knot in the back of his left calf and reached down to prod it with his fingertips, trying to force it to relax. He wiggled his toes, and flashes of pain shot up through the calf as the muscle resisted. Turning his foot, he flexed the calf and ankle, holding his breath against the intense pain.

Rolling on his side, he took the pressure off both legs,

letting them slide out behind him until he lay with his chest on the rocks. He took as much weight as he could on his elbows, but the rock was sharp edged and dug into his ribs and forearms. Peering around the corner of the boulder, he could see the broad shoulders of the point man about forty feet uphill.

The point man froze suddenly, as if he sensed something. Slocum tensed. His weight pinned the Winchester butt between his hip and the rock. He tried to pull it free by shifting his body, but the gun slipped and landed on the rocky ground with a clatter.

The point man spun around and Slocum ducked. He snatched angrily at the carbine, catching it by the barrel and dragging it up to rest it on the boulder again. The point man spotted it and started to move. Slocum sighted hastily and fired, the gun still in midair. The carbine bucked, slamming into his chest, and he nearly doubled over. When he looked up, all three men were out of sight.

Slocum backed away, scrambling into the grass like a confused crab. At least one of them knew where he was now, and the others soon would. He stared hard at the tops of the grass, waiting for some unnatural movement to betray the hidden cowboys. In the distance he heard a hawk, but except for the sighing of the breeze through the tall grass, it was the only sound.

The surface of the grass undulated under the pressure of the wind, but there was no way to tell where the men were. Slocum backed away, taking advantage of the same wind to hide his own movement. He glanced behind him, estimating the distance to the trees. It was a good fifty or sixty yards. No way to make it without leaving his back open to a clear shot.

He dropped to his stomach, pulled the Winchester in tight, and gritted his teeth. He used his legs to set himself rolling downhill. A dozen feet later, his ribs on fire, he lay there panting. His eyes and mouth were full of seed hulls and dead bugs. Brittle wings and prickly seeds cascaded down his collar, sticking to the sweaty skin of his wrists and neck. He itched all over.

Slocum caught his breath and lay still, listening for anything, a whisk of the grass, the thud of a bootheel on the ground, heavy breathing. But it was quiet. He got to his knees, using the Winchester as a lever to get himself upright. He took his hat off and set it on the ground, then poked his head up as high as he dared. The grass waved back and forth across his field of vision.

He could play hide-and-seek all day long, but as long as it was three to one, the odds were definitely against him. He had to do something to draw them out, maybe even startle them into a mistake, but what?

The breeze swept downhill into his face, cooling him a little. The tall grass bent toward him, but he still saw nothing. A scrape, then another, made him cock his head. It sounded like a knife blade on hard wood, an old man whittling on the front porch. After a long pause, he heard it again, still unable to place the sound. The breeze was picking up again, and the sound died away under the steady rustle of the grass.

He nearly missed the first puff of smoke. It shot up like a frightened bird, then vanished as the wind tore it to pieces. Another one, this time a thin column, spiraled up out of the grass, and he realized what was happening.

They were going to try to burn him out.

Instinctively, he grabbed a handful of the grass. It was somewhere between green and yellow, but it was dry. And it would burn. He scrambled backward, less cautious now, as the first whiff of burning grass caught up with him, swirled around his shoulders, then disappeared.

Already the grass had started to crackle, and that distinctive sound, like water rushing over a distant cliff, began to rise behind him. Slocum got to his feet and started to run. Something cracked, and he heard the bullet sail over his head as he turned toward the shot. A wall of thin gray smoke hovered in the air. Even as he watched, two more puffs of smoke spun up and away as the men lit the grass in two more places. The smoke began to thicken, turning darker as he tried to pierce it.

The wind was fairly steady, and there was little chance their gamble would backfire. The heat of the flames, which darted like blue hummingbirds in and out of the grass and smoke, dried the grass around it, curing additional fuel and spreading the fire out in a rough arc. Prodded by the wind, it had begun to move toward him. It seemed to spurt forward, then stall, then squirt ahead again as it waited patiently for the grass to shrivel and curl.

Like a shimmering curtain, the smoke spewed up over the slope, and bright sparks climbed on the heated air, winking like fireflies, then dying away to ash and drifting toward him on the wind. He wasn't gaining on the fire, but he was keeping his distance. He looked desperately from one end to the other, but there was no sign of any of the men. If they were smart, they'd hang at either end, using the smoke as cover, and wait for him to run. They could pick him off at their leisure.

If he gave them the chance.

Slocum stopped and dropped to one knee. He stared into the smoke, the Winchester cocked and ready. From one end of the smoky wall to the other, he strained his eyes for a hint, anything, a thickening of the smoke, a shadow hovering behind it, something to shoot at.

At one end of the smoke screen he saw a clot of darkness, either thicker smoke or something more solid. He sighted carefully, not wanting to give himself away without reason. The smoke wavered, but the shadowy knot did not. Something solid lay behind it. Or someone.

He squeezed slowly, steeling himself for the impact of the Winchester against his shoulder. The carbine barked, and his whole skeleton seemed to rattle within his skin. The clot of darkness disappeared, and he heard someone groan. He aimed lower, and fired again. This time, he heard nothing.

With a bellow, someone charged around the corner of
the wall of flame. The man seemed to be running without
knowing where or why. Slocum fired again, and this time
he knew he'd hit his target. The man stopped in his tracks,
then fell straight down, as if his legs had dissolved beneath
him.

Slocum didn't wait. Spinning on his knee, he stumbled
toward the trees, half running and half crawling. He heard a
shout behind him, then a gun barked twice. The shots sailed
high, whining through the trees. Slocum didn't hesitate.
Reaching the relative safety of the cottonwoods, he ducked
down behind the thickest tree and leaned against it, gasping
for breath.

He couldn't see any of the cowboys as the flames continued to march downhill. He saw the wounded gunman
climb to his feet, a bright red smear high on his shoulder.
He tried to run, but one leg wouldn't hold his weight. He
stumbled and Slocum waited for him to get up again. The
flames drew closer, and Slocum found himself rooting for
the wounded man. But nothing moved on the slope.

The flames seemed to stutter momentarily, as if frozen,
then plunged forward again, advancing with explosive
speed. He heard the man shout, and one arm flailed in the
air. Once again the bloodstained shoulder bobbed into view,
this time not five feet from the flames. The man tried again
to run. And again he fell.

Slocum gimped to the chestnut and hauled himself into
the saddle. Kicking the big horse, he angled through the
trees and back toward the trail. From beyond the trees, he
watched as the two men tried to get to their companion, but
the heat drove them back. They turned and fired at him and,
when their guns were empty, they raised their fists.

The flames danced forward one more time, and Slocum
stopped his ears, turning away until the screaming ended.

19

Slocum tailed the two survivors. He hung back, letting them take a good lead. Their pace was easy, as if they had been traumatized by the death of the point man. Or as if they were the bearers of bad news, and knew what happened to such messengers.

He knew that Mackay was somewhere at the bottom of things, like sludge at the bottom of a barrel. But knowing it and proving it were two vastly different matters. Part of Slocum wanted some final confrontation, in which he could write a finish to Mackay with no doubts at all. But that was just too tidy. Life wasn't that clean and that neat.

They were headed toward the Broken Rail. The largest spread in the county, it was adjacent to Tim Baker's Double Rocker, but nearly twice as big. From what Pete Harney had said, and much that he'd implied, Brett Mackay pretty much had the run of the place. And if it was anything like the Double Rocker, it might take a month to find him, unless the two men ahead of him led him to his quarry.

Sitting on their tails, Slocum was getting impatient. At one point, he considered dropping them, then forcing them to tell him where Mackay was, but it was too risky. If they spotted him before he got close, they'd bolt, and he'd be back to square one. Or they might be more afraid of Mackay than they were of him. They might lie, or even refuse to talk at all. Then he would be leadless, drifting like an empty boat.

It was more frustrating, but ultimately better, to stay calm and follow wherever they led him. Images of the past week kept dancing through his head. He could see the old actor's battered and bleeding face in his lap, that one eye staring up at him, deeper than any pool, full of more pain, and more wisdom, than any he'd ever seen.

He saw Moseley's hand, the way the creek water curled around the bent fingers, catching the light for a moment before plunging on. He could see Portia, standing there in the lamplight, the cascade of red curls over her shoulders.

And he could see Cordelia, the look of complete bafflement on her face as he tried again and again to explain that he'd tried to help her father, not hurt him. Then, backlit by the flash of lightning, the two of them, father and daughter, stumbling through the windswept street that first night.

It was that image that haunted him now, in broad daylight.

Behind him, Slocum saw the plumes of thick black smoke rising up from the grass fire. The smoke hung like a cloud on the horizon, swirling in the rising heat. And up ahead, another kind of cloud. They were heading into the highlands, and the soil was getting rocky. More scrub pines dotted the landscape, and patches of daisies and paintbrush sprouted, their colors even brighter against the beige background.

After two hours, Slocum's legs were beginning to tire.

He was trying to keep his weight on the stirrups to cushion his ribs, but the effort was taking its toll. He reined in just below a ridge and scrambled to the top to watch the two cowhands ride into the mouth of a ravine. He was on the edge of Double Rocker land now, and the territory ahead was unknown. He'd chased a few strays onto the Broken Rail, but not far and not often. He had to keep the men close now, and run the risk of being spotted.

He waited until the riders were out of sight, then remounted and kicked the chestnut up and over the ridge. It would be tricky from here on in. If they'd spotted him already, they could bushwhack him with no trouble. He was on their territory, and they held all the cards. But he was getting too close to the end to pack it in. He hadn't come this far, endured as much as he had, to let one more danger turn him away.

Brett Mackay was out there somewhere, and Brett Mackay was going to pay the piper, come hell or high water.

He hesitated at the ravine mouth, just long enough to hear the steady clomp of two horses somewhere ahead. The ravine floor was rock littered, the ground stony. It showed few tracks, but a hoofprint here and there was all he needed.

The high walls just inside the mouth of the ravine threw deep shadows across its floor. Bright sun glanced off the rocks halfway up the hundred feet of sheer stone. The floor of the cut sloped sharply upward. Ahead he could see how the walls shrank down. Sun spilled over the lip ahead, and he could chart his progress by the shadow line on the wall.

At the far end, he had to dismount again. He crept out of the rocks at the base of the right-hand wall, then up a scree-covered slope. A stand of pines bulked in the left-hand corner, spilling spiky shadows across the narrow mouth.

Behind him, his horse pawed the ground nervously. The trail was clear here, dark, damp earth marking every hoof. The riders had cut left and started down a long pine-filled corridor. High rock walls marked the left edge, and a series of steep six-and eight-foot cliffs stepped down to the valley floor on the right.

Regaining his mount, he followed the trail down through the needle carpet. It had seen some heavy traffic in recent days. Clumps of mushrooms sprouted up through the needles, some newly mashed, others a day or two before judging by the dark pulp they had become. The needles muffled his mount's hooves, but the men ahead of him had the same advantage. The trees were too thick for him to see more than sixty or seventy feet down through their ranks.

He took it easy, letting the chestnut walk the corridor at its own pace. The steep decline started to belly up, and by the time he was halfway down, it had flattened considerably. High rock walls towered up beyond the trees on his left, but the sun was ahead of him and lanced through the trees here and there. The trees started to thin out, and he saw an occasional stump where a tree had been hacked off. A thin plume of smoke spiraled up into the air, turning suddenly transparent when it climbed out of the shade and into the sun.

Slocum dismounted and grabbed the reins, tugging the chestnut into a clump of junipers up against the wall. He tethered the horse and jerked his Winchester out of the boot. He still had the pocketful of shells, and he refilled the magazine, jerked one into the chamber, and started down through the remaining trees.

Behind a thick fir stump, he dropped to the ground to watch the riders cover the last two hundred yards to a mud-wattled log cabin. That explained the stumps. And the smoke. The two men tied their horses next to four others. A figure in jeans and the top half of a pair of long johns appeared in a suddenly open door.

The man was too far away for Slocum to recognize him. None of the horses was familiar, but he didn't know what Mackay was riding. There was only one way to be certain the big cowhand was there. A clear creek, its deep waters occasionally whitened by clusters of granite, wound past the cabin. Lush grass covered the bank on either side. There was no way to get close from here.

Behind the cabin, a steep slope, littered with huge boulders, swept up toward the ridgeline. A grove of blue spruce trees swept past the rear of the building, and if he could get to it somehow, it would cover him to within twenty or twenty-five feet of the cabin. The creek spilled into the valley floor off a sheer rock wall a quarter mile upstream. Anyone on the porch had a clear look at the waterfall, and the rocky edge of the deep pool beneath it, but that was Slocum's only avenue.

He scrambled back to his horse and climbed into the saddle, cradling the Winchester across his thighs. The horse resented climbing back uphill so soon, but Slocum prodded him repeatedly and the chestnut broke into a trot. Threading his way through the pines, he came to a low rise overlooking the waterfall. He looked up, debating whether to go up and around, but it would take too much time, and there was no way he could get back down, as far as he could tell.

Shrugging away the inevitability, he took the chestnut down toward the pool, dismounted, and tethered him in some scrub pine. Slocum ran in a crouch, dodging from rock to rock, until he came to the edge of the cascade pool. He could see the front porch of the cabin clearly, but the front door was closed, and no one was outside. He pressed against the rock, stepping on moss-covered stones, and made his way behind the screen of falling water. The far side was a little trickier.

Once he covered twenty-five yards of open ground he could duck into the spruces, but it was a long sprint in his condition. Taking a deep breath, he ducked as low as he could and broke for the edge of the grove. His chest screamed with his labored breathing, but he made it. From this point on it was clear sailing to a spot directly behind the cabin. As soon as he caught his second wind, he broke into a dogtrot.

The scent of the spruces was sharp, almost sweet, and the thick layer of needles cushioned his feet. He was able to run easily, and covered the quarter mile with little or no pain. He found an opening in the trees and dropped to his belly. Crawling toward the back wall of the cabin, he hesitated on the edge of the grove, watching a long moment.

As he was about to leave the cover, something caught his eye high on the opposite slope. He froze for an instant, then scrambled backward under the lowest branches of a thickly needled spruce. Carpet beetles scurried over his hands as he lay there waiting for the movement to be repeated.

He saw it again, just a shadowy movement toward the front edge of the stand of pines. One, no two, horses bobbed into view, then disappeared again. They were more than halfway down, and he waited patiently, catching a glimpse twice more before they broke into the clear for good.

He wished he had binoculars, but they were in his saddlebags. It was a man and a woman, that much he was sure of, but he couldn't identify either rider. He patted the ground impatiently, then grabbed fistfuls of dried needles, squeezing them to calm himself.

He watched as the approaching riders eased into the creek, then disappeared behind the roof of the cabin. The man was Brett Mackay, there was no doubt about that. But the woman's face had been half hidden behind her hat brim. That part of her face not in shadow was blurred white and featureless by the bright sun. He cursed under his breath.

Now what, dammit? He sighed in exasperation, squeezing the needles even harder, then tossing them away in disgust.

The door slammed on the far side, and he shook his head. This changed things. He had to know who the woman was. And there was no way in hell, no matter who she was, he was going to charge in their with a drawn gun. And, if she was one of Ramsey's daughters, whether there by choice or not, things were going to be just that much stickier.

There was one window in the rear of the cabin. It was curtained with an old burlap sack. As long as no one looked out, he'd be able to get up close. Maybe he'd know what to do once he learned a little more. Sighing again, he crept out from under the spruce. He shook the Winchester to make sure no needles clogged the barrel or the lever action, then started for the back wall of the cabin.

It was the longest fifty feet he could remember. Every nerve was on fire. He could hear his heart pounding in his ears. Every beat sent a tremor through his tender ribs. After what seemed like an eternity, he was close enough to reach out and touch the logs, and he stopped to catch his breath and let his nerves settle down.

Eight people, probably seven of them men, were inside the cabin. Even if he were inclined to suicide, there had to be easier ways than kicking open the front door. He crawled under the window but could hear only a low murmur of voices. He tilted his hat back and raised his head to the level of the sill. A couple of cracks, where the burlap curled away from the inside of the window, let him see into the room, but he saw only parts of bodies. Three pairs of boots, and legs to the knees, were arranged in a semicircle at a round table, probably playing cards.

Other than that he could see nothing. After half an hour he knew nothing more than he knew before. Boots scraped on the floor as people moved back and forth, but he never got a glimpse of a face. He started around the edge of the cabin. A pile of fresh logs, an axe and wedge thrown carelessly on top, blocked his progress. He had started around the woodpile when he heard the door latch creak, followed by boots on the wooden porch.

Slocum ducked back behind the firewood just as someone walked to the edge of the porch. He could see the toes of the man's boots as he stood there and spat off into the grass. "I don't like it, Brett," someone said. "Should have plugged that damn midget, 'stead of just runnin' him off. And you never should have brought that girl here. Christ sakes, I—"

He heard the unmistakable thud of knuckles on meat, and

saw a man sprawl on his back off the porch. The man lay there, glaring, ignoring the trickle of blood and spittle down his chin. "You shouldn't have done that, Mackay."

"Don't tell me what I should do."

"You're gonna get us all hung, you damn fool. All because of some skirt."

"Don't worry, Deak, you won't hang. I'll shoot you first."

"That ain't funny, Brett. It just ain't funny."

"Don't worry about it. I got to go. Make sure you're where I told you. Tonight."

"Where you gonna be?"

"I got to go back to Dry Spring."

The man got up slowly, brushing himself off while still in a crouch. He stepped onto the porch, and a woman's voice said, "Brett, I think maybe this is getting out of control."

"You think so, do you, honey? Well, let me tell you, I'm gonna make sure it ain't. I'll handle it, like I told you I would."

"I don't think it's a good idea."

"Honey, ain't you learned nothing all them years roamin' around the country? Women ain't supposed to think. They supposed to just lie back and enjoy it. Let the men do the work."

"You're a pig."

"Maybe so, darlin', maybe so. But I bring home the bacon, and that's a fact. Now, get on your horse and don't argue with me no more. You hired me to do a job, and I'm gonna do it. 'Sides, it ain't work no more. It's personal now."

"But—" She stopped as something that could only have been a smack jolted her. Slocum could hear plainly the sound of her teeth snapping together.

"Now git on your horse," Mackay snarled.

20

Slocum backed away from the cabin. He could hear the squeak of leather as Mackay and the woman climbed into the saddle. Ducking into the spruce grove, he sprinted back toward the waterfall, using the carbine to brush branches aside. As he reached the edge of the pool, the two riders were already out of sight.

A man stood on the porch, staring up into the trees, watching the riders. As Slocum stepped into the open, the man turned, glanced toward the waterfall, then disappeared behind the edge of the cabin. Slocum held his breath, uncertain whether he had been seen.

But there was no time to play it cautious. If he lost Mackay now, he'd have no way to stop whatever it was that was supposed to happen. Keeping low, he danced through the boulders and took the slippery rocks behind the waterfall so fast there wasn't time to lose his footing. He nearly fell as he made the last long leap to solid ground on the far side. Landing on one knee, he braced himself with an outstretched arm and dropped the Winchester.

As he bent to retrieve it, a bullet slammed into the rock, just over his head. They had seen him after all. He glanced toward the cabin but saw no one. A second shot ricocheted off the same rock, then whistled past him on the rebound. He ducked for cover, using the Winchester as a cane. Pulling himself from rock to rock, he tore his knees up on the sharp stone slivers littering the ground.

He could see the horse, but he had thirty yards of dead clear air to get through to the nearest cover. So far, the shooter had shown little sign of marksmanship. But if the War Between the States had taught him anything, it was that even an accidental hit could kill you.

The horse shied away, tugging the reins loose and backing away from the clearing. Slocum whistled to it, but the animal was too skittish to respond. If the horse bolted, he was in deep water. He waited for the third shot. Counting the seconds, he reached sixty, then one-twenty. Two minutes was patience enough, and he dashed into the clearing. With every step, he waited for a bullet to rip through him. Zigzagging was all but pointless. He was running straight across the rifleman's sights, and the sooner he got into the trees, the safer he would be.

Halfway across, there was still no indication of another shot. By the time he reached the three-quarter mark, he knew there wouldn't be one. He didn't look back until he stumbled and fell on his face at the edge of the trees. Grinding his cheek into the prickly carpet of needles, he stared downhill for a long moment, when he spotted three men on horseback, already beginning the long sprint up the creekbank. They were in full gallop as he got to his feet and darted among the broad trunks of the pines.

Slocum dropped to one knee and swung the Winchester

around. He sighted hastily, pulling the trigger as soon as he caught the first glimpse of movements behind the iron nib. The shot sank a little on the downhill trajectory. The lead horse stumbled, its rider spilling headlong, one foot still in a stirrup as the horse tried to stand. It bucked and swung sideways, dragging the rider a half-dozen yards.

The remaining horsemen slowed their charge as Slocum got up to run. Both riders fired wildly. Their revolvers were all but useless at that range, and they seemed uncertain whether to go back to help their mate or push on after their quarry. Slocum took advantage of the confusion to mount up. He pushed his horse into a full gallop, swinging the Winchester back over his shoulder and trying to brace it as the chestnut bounced uphill.

Slocum fired once, then booted the carbine and turned his attention to the treacherous ascent. The trees flashed by on either side, and he was forced to jerk the reins from time to time to avoid a particularly low-hanging branch. He couldn't tell whether he was being followed, but he had enough to deal with for the moment.

And up ahead, there remained the possibility that Mackay had heard the firing and had either stopped to see what had happened or might even have doubled back. Either way, Slocum knew he could be riding straight up a gun barrel. And he wouldn't know it until it was useless knowledge.

He headed for the sun, already beginning to sink. It was turning a blue gray under the trees, as purple washed over the rock and glanced through the pines. Sunset was still a couple of hours away, but the ravine ahead would be full of shadows. Even in bright sunlight it offered more than enough places to mount a decent ambush. With the added edge of poor visibility, a waiting gunman could toast marshmallows with one hand and hold off a dozen Sioux with the other. The only question in Slocum's mind was whether it was worth it to Mackay to waste his time.

He cleared the last few trees and reined in hard. Dismounting, he listened to the slope below him, but heard no signs of pursuit. He tugged on the reins and dragged the horse uphill toward the opening into the ravine. His boots slipped on the loose soil, and he was forced to dig his heels in with every step to keep from sliding back downhill.

The horse jerked incessantly, making the climb just that much tougher. Slocum debated whether to take the more direct ravine route back to Dry Spring. Time was the only reason, and since he didn't know how much he had, it was a strong argument. But on the other hand, he told himself, all the time in the world won't help a dead man.

He hated to do it, but it seemed the only sensible thing to do. Regaining the saddle, he pushed the horse on past the ravine entrance, letting the chestnut pick its way up the steep slope to the cliffs above the ravine. He could look down into the shadow-filled canyon, but saw little but clumps of gray rock in pools of blue-black darkness over half the ravine floor. The reflected light spilling into the other half was almost as useless. The ravine appeared deserted, and he didn't have the time to make more than a cursory examination.

He followed the edge of the ravine as closely as he dared. The rocks made his course anything but direct, and he didn't want to come close enough to present a target to anyone on the floor below. Having committed to the high road, there was nothing at all to gain by caution. He was already fifteen or twenty minutes behind Mackay, and the more time he wasted, the bigger the cowboy's lead became.

It took him almost an hour to reach the far end of the ravine. As he started the treacherous descent, he kept an eye open for any sign of Mackay and the woman, but the cloudless sky, now starting to darken a bit as the sun sank behind him, was perfectly quiet. As far as he could see, not a bird rose up in fright. He heard nothing, not even a sudden hiss of grass as a spooked rabbit ran for cover. He and the horse could almost be the only living things for miles ahead.

Getting down was tougher than getting up, and he sawed

the reins to force the chestnut into an improvised series of cutbacks. He kept the angle as flat as he could until the ground started to level out after the sixth change of direction. He kept watching the sky far out across the valley floor, but it stayed as calm and empty as it had been.

If Mackay was out there, he was far ahead. If he wasn't, then he was long gone and Siocum was altogether without a clue. The grass rolled endlessly, prodded by a stiffening breeze. The closer he came to the valley floor, the thicker the grass became. It rustled in the wind, filling the air with a steady hissing as its blades slashed at one another in an endless duel.

When he hit the bottom of the loose scree, he spurred the big chestnut into a flat-out gallop. The only thing he could do was head straight for Dry Spring. He was convinced that, whatever Mackay had in mind, it would happen in town.

The big horse moved almost effortlessly now. It seemed to be relieved not to deal with the treacherous footing of the slope. It barely slowed as they started back uphill. As he rode, Slocum sorted through his options. They were damn few, and none seemed very promising.

He could watch the theater tent, on the off chance that Mackay planned another attack during the performance. He could hunt Mackay down and take him out, worrying about reasons later. Or he could go straight to Ray Castle, tell him what he knew and what he'd learned from Harney, and wash his hands of the whole affair. None of his choices was both practical and acceptable. Castle would laugh him out of town, and that would accomplish nothing.

Taking on Mackay on his own was asking for a murder charge if he had to kill the man, which was all but certain. Or, worse yet, he could get himself killed, leaving Ramsey at the cowboy's mercy. That wouldn't accomplish a hell of a lot either.

That left sitting on his hands, letting Mackay have the first move. But something told him the first move might be all Mackay needed. That, too, seemed worthless.

He was staring at a royal flush with a hand full of nothing.

Slocum watched the sun recede as if it were an enemy. His shadow speared out ahead of him. The longer it got, the closer he got to despair.

And nagging at the back of his mind was the identity of the woman with Mackay. He couldn't tell for sure, but it almost had to be one of Ramsey's daughters. There was no way in hell it could have been Cordelia, but that's as far as he could go with any certainty. No matter which way he looked at it, the choices were narrowed to two. It had to be either Portia or Juliet. If it was Portia, he'd been made a bigger fool the second time around. If it was Juliet, it wouldn't be much better. You can't defend a fort as long as someone on the inside is willing to open the gates.

It said little for Juliet, and less for Portia, that he couldn't rule either of them out. And every time he thought of that foolish old man, lying there with one eye swollen shut, his face a mass of bloody lumps, he wanted to shoot someone. He just wasn't sure whom. Mackay, yes, of course, but wasn't a traitor worse than a bully? Didn't someone in the professor's camp make it all possible?

It was past sundown when he saw the tent rise up ahead of him like a mirage. It seemed to float in the air a half-dozen feet above the ground as he raced toward it. The performance, if Ramsey was even capable of going on, was less than an hour away. There was just too damn little time to do everything he had to do.

He spurred the chestnut even harder, watching the tent bob up and down like a rudderless ship tossed about by the waves. It looked deserted from long range, and the closer he got, the more ominous seemed its desertion. He knew the troupe could find a way to go on without Ramsey, but the old man was the heart and soul, the brains and the guts, of the company. If he was unable to go on, there was no one to take up the slack. Not even Cordelia could galvanize the others the way her father did.

He skidded to a halt beside the tent and let the reins drag on the ground as he dismounted and loped for Ramsey's wagon. He knocked once, then a second time before climbing the stairs. He pushed through the makeshift curtain. A single lamp, pale to the point of darkness, bathed the wagon in thick amber light. Ramsey lay on his cot, a thick compress on his forehead. He seemed to be sleeping. Asleep in a chair beside him sat Cordelia. She was in costume, ready to go on as a witch in the opening scene, but Ramsey himself wore only a nightshirt.

Slocum dropped to his knees and shook Cordelia gently by the shoulder.

She jerked awake, her eyes suddenly huge as saucers as she stared at him. "God, you startled me." Her voice was hoarse, her lips pasty and sticking together as she tried to speak.

"How is he?"

"Not good. His face looks terrible. He keeps falling asleep, and I can't wake him without a struggle."

"Have you had the doctor in to look at him?"

"Yes . . . " She shrugged. "He says Daddy needs to rest. There is nothing permanently wrong, but he's frail. He took a terrible beating."

Slocum nodded. "Anything I can do?"

She shook her head.

"You're not going to put on the play tonight, are you?"

"Of course we are." She seemed amazed he would even consider anything less. "Winston will take Daddy's part."

"Maybe that's not such a good idea."

"It's the only idea, Mr. Slocum. It is the only idea."

He stood up, ducking his head a little under the low roof. "Alright, I guess you know what's best."

She stared at him for a long time. "Is there anything you want to say?"

"No, I don't guess there is."

"Fine. Then whatever happens happens."

"Yes. Whatever happens happens. Is your sister here?"

"Which one? Or aren't you particular?" She stared at him with undisguised contempt.

"It's not what you think. I just want to know, that's all."

"Why?"

"Just answer the question."

"I don't know. I've been here all afternoon. I no longer care what either of them does. They are adept at making their own beds. Now they will have to learn to lie in them."

Slocum exhaled sharply.

"You needn't be so contemptuous of me, Mr. Slocum."

He stepped to the doorway. Taking the blanket in one hand, he bunched it and pushed it aside, letting in a burst of cool air from outside. He looked at her for a moment in silence. Then, almost as an afterthought, he said, "That's what you think."

21

Slocum paced nervously during the last act. The play had gone off without a hitch. The audience was quiet, and there had been no sign of Mackay or any of his friends. It was beginning to look as if nothing would happen. It was hot in the tent, and Slocum stepped outside to get some fresh air. He lit a cigarette and strolled around the perimeter of the canvas, stepping over the pegs that held it down every few paces.

It was a clear night, and he watched the stars for a minute. There were times when he envied the sky its peacefulness. Everything in its place and a place for everything. That was the way the world should be, the way it would be if it weren't for Mackay and his ilk. But it only took one. He remembered his grandmother, all those damn sayings,

"One bad apple," and so on. It was a shame she had been so right.

As he completed his trip around the tent, Pete Harney stepped through the opening. "Johnny, too much drama for you, too, huh?"

Slocum smiled inwardly. Harney should only know. But he wouldn't tell him anything. Not yet, anyway. "I guess a little culture goes a longer way than I'm prepared to go," he said.

Harney laughed. "You don't fool me, John. You wouldn't be here at all if the professor had ugly daughters."

"You do me an injustice, sir," Slocum said, declaiming in a fair parody of the old actor.

"He's one tough old bird, isn't he?"

"I'm not so sure, Pete. I'm not so sure."

"Well, it's just a few more days and he'll move on. I guess we've seen the last of Mr. Mackay for a while, too. That was some thrashing you gave him."

"He had it coming."

"Oh, I know he did. Don't get me wrong. I'm not saying you shouldn't have. Fact is, some folks around town are kinda sorry you stopped when you did."

"I didn't decide that on my own, Pete. But I hate being out of control like that. It's just as well somebody did stop me. I got a feeling Ray Castle wouldn't be as lazy in looking for me as he is chasing whoever killed Moseley."

"You can't blame Ray. Hell, who's he supposed to look for? Nobody saw it happen. There's no way in hell to prove anything."

"That doesn't mean he shouldn't try, Pete."

"I know it. I know that. But . . . " He spread his hands in a gesture of helplessness. "Some things ain't fair. That's all there is to it."

A burst of applause signaled the end of the play, and Harney stepped aside as people started to file out. Slocum watched the audience break into small clumps. Harney chatted amiably with a couple of small ranchers. He wanted to introduce Slocum, who begged off, saying he was going back to the hotel. He started off and Paddy Gibson caught up with him.

"Johnny," he said, "guess you're the local peacemaker. Nice crowd tonight. No trouble at all. Word must have got around that you were riding herd."

Slocum flashed a quick smile. "I wish it could be that simple, Paddy."

"You coming back soon? Mr. Baker is getting antsy."

"I'll be back in a couple of days. Soon as my ribs toughen up a little."

"Didn't look so bad last night. I'll bet old Brett will agree with that, too."

Slocum didn't answer.

"Buy you a drink, Johnny?"

"No, thanks, Paddy. I'm still a little under the weather. Think I'll just turn in."

Gibson ducked into the Pinon as they passed by, and Slocum continued on to the hotel. Harney shouted something to him, but he just turned and waved good night. He didn't relax until he was in his room.

He felt drained, as if every last bit of energy had been sapped somehow. He wanted to sleep and wished he could sleep for a week. He lay on the bed, tossing one edge of a blanket over his legs, and stared at the ceiling. The noise of departing theatergoers gradually died down, dwindling to an occasional horse or two, a creaking wagon. Soon that, too, was gone.

The room was stuffy, and he opened his window, then lay back down. He could hear the sound of Paddy's piano, little tinkly scraps carried on the breeze, not enough even to recognize a tune.

Eventually the piano, too, stopped. He hadn't slept a wink, and didn't have any idea of the time. Tossing and turning, he tried every conceivable combination of man and mattress, but sleep refused to come. He got up and pulled the curtain aside. Looking up at the sky, he watched a single cloud scud by on a stiff wind. He followed it until it was out of sight, then let the curtain fall and walked back to the bed.

Sitting on the edge of the mattress, he tapped one foot on the floor. He felt as if his skin were full of writhing snakes. Every muscle jumped or twitched. He took a deep breath, and something bit at his nostrils. He sniffed now, then moved back to the window. He smelled something. As he leaned back toward the open window, a woman screamed. There was no mistaking it. Something was burning.

Craning his head out the window, he looked as far as he could down the street, but he saw nothing. He grabbed his gunbelt and started down the hall as he strapped it on. Taking the stairs two at a time, he bounded into the lobby. The night clerk was heading toward the front door at the same time.

"You hear that?" the clerk asked.

Slocum nodded, pushing the young man aside and jerking the door open. Out in the street, he spotted four or five people leaning out their windows.

"That way," one of them shouted, "down there. Fire . . . " Slocum started up the center of the street. He didn't have to see it to know what was burning. Even as he broke into a run, he saw the thick black smoke curling over the theater tent. He was still a block away when the first flames licked up along the canvas.

Other people were dashing into the streets, and Slocum ran as fast as his ribs allowed. He could see the flames clearly now as they licked toward him around the far edge of the tent. An ugly orange, they spewed thick black smoke in clots and tendrils.

Another burst of flame, then a third, came from two of the wagons. Members of the troupe ran in circles, not knowing what to do. Half of the tent was a solid sheet of flame now, already turning to ash and starting to drift on the heated air. The sky was full of orange and black stars now as the pall of smoke blotted out the sky.

Slocum ran for Ramsey's wagon, one of the two set on fire. He leaped up the steps and found Cordelia struggling to drag her father from his cot. The old man tried to fight her off.

"No, let me burn," he shouted. "Let me burn, damn you. It's what you all want." He slapped Cordelia, and sent her reeling into the side of the wagon.

Slocum caught her before she fell and hurried her outside. "I'll get him," he said. "You stay outside. I'll get him."

The canvas roof of the wagon had started to burn, and tongues of flame licked at the edges of charred holes in the top as Slocum grabbed Ramsey under the arms.

The old man rolled into a ball, kicking at Slocum with one naked foot.

"Leave me alone, damn you. Leave me alone."

"Professor, you have to get out. You can't stay here."

"Get out, get ouuuuttt." The last was like an animal howl, and it sent shivers up Slocum's spine.

He wrapped the old man in his arms and picked him up bodily. Ramsey twisted and turned like an angry five-year-old. He swung at Slocum with one frail fist, but the blows did no damage. Ramsey was too weak to hurt anyone but himself. Slocum stumbled toward the tail of the wagon, ducking under the iron frame as half of the canvas above him burst into flame with a loud pop, like a flag flapping in a stiff breeze.

Using Ramsey's head and shoulder to push the blanket aside, he groped for the first step. His eyes burned, and every breath felt like hot lead poured down his throat. He lost his balance on the final step and stumbled, but someone caught him by the shoulder. "I got him, Johnny, let me have him."

"Pete?"

"You better sit down, boyo."

Slocum felt the burden shift, then Ramsey was gone, and only the smoke pressed on his chest. He coughed, nearly throwing up. He staggered like a drunk and rubbed his eyes with ashy knuckles.

Blinking away the pain, he saw the tent start to sag. The supporting ropes had begun to part, and the flaming canvas sagged in toward the center pole. Flames swirled around the thick timber. In the garish light, Slocum could see the snapped cables, themselves burning like sluggish fuses.

The townspeople were forming a bucket brigade. A ragged line snaked toward a horse trough. Two men worked the pump, filling the trough and buckets when they were available. The tent was a lost cause, and the water doused the flames on the two wagons first. The actors fell into the line as it coiled toward the ruined tent like a spastic rattler.

There was no way to get the water high enough to put out all the flames, and two men on horseback tried to get a rope over the top of the tent pole. They managed to snag it, then backed their horses, tugging the pole away from the nearest building at the end of the street. Its roof was littered already with glowing ashes and scraps of burning canvas.

The pole began to yield. It creaked and groaned as another man sawed away at the ropes on the unburned half. The ropes snapped one by one, and the pole tilted far over until, with the horses straining, it finally gave way altogether and landed with a loud thud.

The brigade forked into two ends, one dousing the roof of the threatened building, the other drenching the remaining canvas and the ruined props. The whole ashen mass jutted up here and there where props and the undamaged portion of the stage itself kept the canvas off the ground.

Slocum left the line as the flames winked out, leaving the others to soak the embers. Pushing through the crowd, he found one of the actors, Moseley's friend, standing and wringing his hands.

"Where's Professor Ramsey?"

"I don't know." The kid was stunned into stupidity. He

kept staring at the ruins, his lips flapping like the gills of a landed trout. "I don't know," he croaked again.

Slocum looked for Cordelia and couldn't see her. He went to one of the undamaged wagons and pulled the curtain aside without climbing the steps. "Professor?"

"He's here." It was Portia.

Slocum climbed into the wagon. His eyes still burned, and it was difficult to see in the dim lamplight. "You better bring him to the hotel," he said. "He can have my room. All four of you better—"

"No!" It was Ramsey himself. The old man tried to sit up. "No, I won't leave here. This is my life in ruins. I won't leave. It's all I have."

"Professor, you can't—"

The old man's thunder interrupted him. "Don't tell me what I can do. I am staying. You take the girls."

"We can't leave you, Daddy," Cordelia said. "Mr. Slocum is right. Please, let us take you to the hotel."

The old man stiffened, digging his hands into the mattress and hanging on. He shook his head.

Cordelia looked at Slocum helplessly.

"You go, Cory. I'll stay with him."

Cordelia glared at her sister. "You think you can make up for things now? It's too late for that."

Slocum heard the slap before he realized Portia had moved. "Damn you!" she shouted. "You're so perfect. You're so goddamned perfect, you're a saint, aren't you?"

Cordelia was stunned. "No, I—"

"Go, damn it. Even a saint forgives."

"I'm sorry, I . . . we shouldn't be fighting among ourselves. Not now. I just—"

"Damn it, just go."

Cordelia backed away from the cot. She reached out a hand, blindly, and Slocum took it in his own.

"Come on," he whispered. "Give her a chance."

22

Slocum slept on the floor. He lay there listening to Cordelia toss and turn. It was obvious neither of them was going to get any sleep. But it was equally obvious that there was nothing he could say to her that would change anything that had happened. The theater was in shambles. Her father, his body already broken, seemed on the verge of losing his mind as well. And for what?

Portia had told him some of it, guessed at other parts. But she knew only her own reasons. Why Juliet had taken her role in the affair she could only speculate. And Cordelia had infuriated both of her sisters by insisting on backing her father, no matter what. It seemed willful, even spiteful of her. But she would not back down, and she would not explain.

And now, everything was in ruins. Lives, a family business, perhaps even a family itself. Slocum wondered at the depth of bitterness in Cordelia. How could so young a woman harbor so much resentment? And why would she not explain, not even to those who bore the brunt of it?

Intriguing questions, but he would not ask them. The answers were not his business.

Cordelia was sobbing to herself, doing her best to muffle the sound. Slocum sat up, watching silently. Her shoulders heaved, and the bed shook, but she was not going to let it take control of her. She was angry, and she was hurt, but there was more to her unhappiness than just an argument or the fire. It was deeper than that, and older. Something buried so far inside her that maybe she didn't know herself what it was.

Slocum leaned back against the bed, letting his head rest on the mattress. He sat there for an hour, listening to Cordelia cry, and he couldn't bring himself to make a single sound. She seemed beyond comforting, and would not accept it from him, of all people, in any case. There was nothing else he could do.

As the sun started to come up, he watched bands of light change colors. The wall reddened, then turned pink, and finally exploded as the first clear shafts of sunlight slipped past the curtains. He walked to the window in his stockinged feet and leaned out, balling the curtain in one fist and leaning on the sill. The morning gave no hint of what had happened just a few hours before. The scent of smoke still lingered, but he had to search for it. The sky was a blue so pure it looked as if it would never again be marred by a cloud.

When he let the curtain fall, he turned to find Cordelia sitting up, watching him.

"Morning," he said.

She didn't answer.

"You didn't sleep much," he said.

"No."

"I can get some breakfast for you, if you like."

"I'm not hungry."

"Alright."

"Sit down, Mr. Slocum. I need to talk to someone, and since you're the only one here, it might as well be you."

"You don't owe me any explanations."

"I know that. But I've been very wrong about you. And every time something happens, you do something to make that clearer. You saved my father's life last night. I never could have gotten him out of there by myself."

"It could have been anyone. The professor isn't much of a fighter."

"That's what you think." She stared at him so long that he thought she might have finished. He started to open his mouth, but she held up a finger. "Wait. I just don't know where to begin. I—"

"Forget about it. It's finished now anyway."

"Not quite, Mr. Slocum. Not quite." She started to cry soundlessly, great tears welling in her eyes, then trickling down her cheeks. She wiped at the first one, then surrendered to them. She sat with her hands in her lap. He could see the tears splashing on her hands. She stared at them, but made no attempt to wipe them away. When she started to speak it was as if she were addressing her hands, or the tears themselves.

"My father is dying, Mr. Slocum. He's wasting away, and there's nothing anyone can do about it. He didn't use to be so frail. But he won't stop, he won't even slow down. That's why it's so hateful of my sisters to try and take the theater away from him. It's the only thing he has left, the thing he loves most, now that Mother is gone. . . . "

"I'm sorry. I didn't know."

"No one does. No one except me and his doctor."

"You mean Portia and Juliet don't know?"

"No, they don't know. He didn't want them to know. He didn't want me to know either, but I found out. It doesn't matter how. He made me promise not to tell them."

"How long?"

"Six months, maybe less. No one really knows."

"Why do your sisters want him to sell the theater?"

"Because he had an offer a few months ago. It wasn't anything much, but Daddy likes to talk, and every time he talked about it, the number got higher. Another offer, two people bidding against one another. And the price went up and up. They believed him, because they wanted to believe him. They wanted out. And neither one of them wanted to believe there was nothing much to sell."

"You know Portia is sorry, don't you?"

"No, I don't know that." She came to life suddenly. "I know she probably told you that, but she's never sorry about anything. Maybe that's why I hate her. Maybe I'm jealous. Maybe, just once in my life, I'd like to do something I *should* feel sorry about."

"This time you're wrong. She told me all about it. Told me why, too. That's why her husband left. She wanted to put an end to it, but he wouldn't listen. When she insisted, he left. Where Juliet stands, I'm not so sure. But I believe Portia. Not at first. But I do now."

"And you believe her because you want to. You went to bed with her, and you want to believe she meant that, too. Men are such children . . . such damned idiots."

"Where were your sisters yesterday afternoon?"

"Portia? She was here. We were painting a couple of flats. Daddy wanted some of the scenery redone. I didn't see her much. I stayed with Daddy most of the time. But the flats were all finished, and she's the only one beside me who really knows how to do them."

Slocum nodded. "What about Juliet? Was she here, too?"

"Why do you ask?"

"No reason. Just curious, I guess."

"Don't lie to me, Slocum. You asked for a reason. What was it?"

"Nothing that concerns you."

"If it concerns my family, even my sisters, maybe especially my sisters, it concerns me."

"So ask them about it."

"What's going on, Mr. Slocum?"

"I'm not sure I know."

"But you think you know, don't you? You think you know, and my sisters are involved. Aren't they? Answer me, damn you."

Slocum walked back to the window. "I think I'll look in on your father. You want to come with me?"

"Of course I—"

The hammering on the door drowned out her last words.

"Who is it?" Slocum called.

"It's me. Hurry, please, open the door."

Portia stood in the doorway, gasping for air.

"What's wrong? What's happened to Daddy?"

"Cory, he's gone."

"What?" Slocum pulled her into the room. "What happened?" he asked.

"Daddy's disappeared. I looked everywhere, and no one knows where he is. He's not in his wagon. Somebody said they thought they saw him walking past one of the wagons, but . . ."

"We better go find him," Slocum said. "He's in no condition to go wandering around."

He left the women to fend for themselves and raced down the stairs for the second time that morning. Instead of running to the wagons, this time he sprinted to the livery stable for his horse. He saddled up in a hurry and hit the street at a full gallop.

As he raced through the town he passed the sisters, without slowing down. At the wagons, he dismounted and went from wagon to wagon, asking everyone if they had a clue as to where Ramsey had gone.

The troupers seemed dazed, as if the events of the past forty-eight hours had somehow wiped their minds blank. They stared at Slocum one by one, shook their heads, then followed him with saucer eyes as he moved on to the next blank stare and the one after that. Poking his head into one of the wagons, he saw Juliet sitting with her head bowed, her hands in her lap.

"Where's your father?" Slocum demanded.

"I don't know." She wore the same vacant look. In the dim light of the wagon's interior, it seemed almost like a death mask. Her eyes didn't seem to blink. She raised her head a little to see him more clearly. "Why don't you leave us alone?"

"I saw you yesterday," Slocum said, entering the wagon. "With Mackay."

"No, I—"

"Where's your husband? Is he with Mackay?"

"Denver. He, unh . . . He's gone to Denver, to . . . " She trailed off, her words slowly drying up like a desert spring. She stared at him dumbly, her lips quivering, her hands shaking a little in her lap.

"What were you doing with Mackay?"

"None of your business. None of this is any of your business. It's your fault now. All of it. If you had just gone away, minded your own business . . . I could have handled it. Dan and I, we could have . . . "

"Could have what? You think Mackay is in this for a lousy fifty dollars and a roll in the hay?"

Her head jerked as if she'd been hit. "How did you know that?"

"I heard you, that night I stayed in the wagon. I didn't know it was you, not until yesterday. But I do now."

"It doesn't matter. It's all gone."

"It does matter. Your father's still alive. But he won't last long. If you know where he is, you better tell me. Now!"

"I don't know."

"Did Mackay take him someplace, maybe to that cabin, someplace else you know about?"

She shook her head.

Slocum turned away in disgust. He didn't know whether to believe her or not. But there was no time to waste, and if she was telling the truth, he might just as well get a move on. If she was lying, there was no guarantee he could convince her to talk.

He stepped out of the wagon, half expecting her to stop him. He hesitated on the bottom step, but Juliet said nothing, and he shook his head. As he walked back to his horse, he thought about how little chance he had to find one needle-thin old man in so huge a haystack as Colorado.

As he climbed into the saddle, he saw Portia and Cordelia watching him. He shook his head, and Cordelia turned away. Portia covered her face with her hands.

It was up to him now.

23

Ramsey couldn't have gone far. Slocum leapt into the saddle and galloped out into the flatland surrounding Dry Spring. The ground was dry, and the old man didn't weigh very much. Tracks might be hard to come by. He had to hope he found him before nightfall. In Ramsey's condition, one night would be enough to kill him.

And in the back of his mind, Juliet's attack kept nagging at him. It seemed almost as if she were anxious for an end to things. Just as Slocum was. But there was no trace of remorse in her face. His meddling was little more than prolonging the inevitable. He knew that now, and yet it didn't make a difference.

Ramsey had lived long enough to deserve better. He was entitled to die the way he wanted to, and no one was willing to let that happen. No one, that is, except Cordelia. They were all meddlers in an old man's final weeks, as if his frailty gave them the right. Juliet was greedy, Portia was greedy, or had been, and it was probably too late for that to change, and their husbands were greedy. And even Cordelia was greedy in her own way. They all wanted what they wanted, and to hell with anyone who disagreed.

Slocum stared up at the overpowering sun, knowing that it would sap Ramsey's strength as quickly as any desert. The old man had taken nothing with him, not even water. And in his weakened state, he would not be able to travel too far. But after an hour, zigzagging back and forth, in ever widening arcs, there was still no trace of the old man.

It was a wonder he had managed to get this far, and yet there wasn't a sign that he had even come this way, let alone started to run out of steam. On the next ridge, Slocum reined in. He jerked binoculars from his saddlebags and scanned the downslope, but he saw nothing.

Watching the sky, he realized he was expecting buzzards. It was gruesome, but there was no way to avoid the possibility that the scavengers might be his only lead. One bird, circling high above him, was too far away for him to be sure, but it appeared to be an eagle. Its flight was less agitated than a buzzard's and the bird was making no attempt to circle lower.

If he was going to find the old man, he would need more luck than the day had given him.

By noon, Slocum was starting to think he'd been misled. It was almost inconceivable that Ramsey could have gotten this far, at least without help. He slipped out of the saddle to get a closer look at the ground. Leading the big chestnut by its reins, he walked slowly across a ridgeline, where the vegetation was thinner. He saw no evidence of hoofprints for more than twenty minutes.

When he finally found a set, he wondered whether Ramsey could have come this far. The prints could have belonged to anyone, he knew, but what else could he do?

He could walk all the way to California and not find a trace of one old man on horseback.

Swinging back into the saddle, he prodded the animal with his spurs and started down the slope. Here and there, he saw another hoofprint or two.

Using the glasses again, he scanned the valley floor for some sign of human life. But there was none. Ramsey or not, the rider was out of sight. In the dry earth, the prints had kicked up a little moisture, meaning they were fairly fresh. Whoever was aboard was not in a hurry, which meant that he or she couldn't have gone too far. It seemed like a very slender thread on which to hang anything, but when you have no rope, you use what's available.

Slocum followed the tracks at a trot, slowing now and then to make sure he still had the trail. The rider had never changed pace, almost as if he were being carried rather than directing the mount. That might mean it was Ramsey, but it could also mean it was some farmer out for a ride, or a schoolkid playing hookey.

As he started up the next rise, he was all but ready to pack it in. If he saw nothing from the top of the ridge, he was going to turn back. For all he knew, Ramsey could already have found his way home.

At the top of the steep hill he stood in the saddle, the glasses in one hand. To the naked eye, the next valley was deserted. With glasses, he saw little to change his mind. He let the glasses fall to dangle on the leather strap, and jerked the reins when he heard a gunshot. It was a pistol, but it came from so far away he wasn't quite sure where.

Sitting still, he waited for another shot, but there wasn't a sound. He grabbed the glasses again, looking for something, anything at all, to tell him more than he knew. Again sweeping the valley floor, following the winding course of a broad, sluggish creek studded with trees and clumps of brush, he came up empty. As he was about to let the glasses go, something caught his eye just off the edge of one lens. He moved the glasses slightly, but couldn't find anything. Waiting patiently, he finally saw another movement. It was hard to tell what it was, even through the binoculars.

Again he waited, holding the glasses as steady as possible. He even held his breath for fear of missing some tiny movement. Then, as if shot from a cannon, a horse bolted out of the brush down along the creek. Twiddling the focus, he watched the animal charge uphill toward him for two hundred yards, then stand stock-still. The horse seemed confused and frightened.

Slocum eased his mount down the slope, hoping the riderless horse wouldn't bolt again. He let his horse have its head, and they closed at a fast walk. The riderless mount sported a saddle, but at this range, it was impossible to see any more than that.

As they drew closer, the horse pricked up its ears, tossing its head and knickering, but it made no attempt to run. Slocum dismounted for the last fifty yards, leading his own horse and talking in a low voice to the frightened animal below him. The horse watched him closely, shaking his head and fixing Slocum with its big eyes.

When he was ten feet away, he dropped to his haunches and coaxed the animal toward him, still hanging on to his own mount by the reins. The horse took a tentative step or two, but came no closer.

"Steady, boy," Slocum cooed, reaching one hand out toward the dangling reins as he crept forward on his knees. When his hands closed over the leather, he stood up slowly, stepping toward the horse and patting its neck. The horse shied once, then settled down, as if relieved to be under someone's control again.

Slocum let his own reins go and walked around the empty saddle. There was no sign of blood. The horse was fresh, not even sweating. It had either been resting awhile, or hadn't come very far to begin with. It bent to chomp at the grass as Slocum made a complete circuit, patting its flanks and talking in a soothing monotone.

Looking downhill, toward the brush, he still saw nothing. Hanging on to the reins, he led the animal toward his own mount, climbed into the saddle, and looped the stray's reins around his saddle horn. Nudging the chestnut with his knees, he moved downhill, toward the creek. Not knowing what to expect, he loosened the Colt Navy in his holster, just in case.

Angling toward the broken clumps of brush, he dropped to his feet again. Tying both horses to the brush, he called, "Hello?"

No one answered. "Professor Ramsey, you here?" he called again. But when he listened, all he could hear was the burble of the creek.

Slocum drew his pistol and pushed the branches aside. Easing in toward the water, he stopped every few steps to listen. When he reached the creekbank, he called again, and again no one answered. He headed upstream, hefting the Colt in his right hand, his ears cocked for the slightest sound.

After fifteen feet, he stopped again. Again he shouted Ramsey's name to no avail. As he took another step, he heard the unmistakable sound of a pistol being cocked. He dropped to the ground, straining to get a better sense of direction. There was no further sound, and he started worming his way under the low-hanging branches of some scrub, using his feet to push him ahead.

When he reached the far side of a dense path of brush, he could see into a small clearing. Clayton Ramsey sat with his back against a tree. He held a pistol in his left hand, and Slocum could see that its hammer was cocked. The barrel of the pistol was in Ramsey's mouth.

He wanted to shout, but if he startled the old man, the gun might go off. "Professor," he whispered. "Professor Ramsey . . . "

The old actor looked around, leaving the gun in his mouth, his finger resting lightly on the trigger. Slocum waved a hand and caught the old man's eye. Ramsey stared at the hand a moment, but made no move to put the gun down. Slocum crawled forward a few feet, just enough to straighten up.

"Put the gun down, Professor, please."

Ramsey shook his head with a violence that amazed him. "Don't be foolish, Professor," Slocum pleaded.

Ramsey smiled a strange smile, his thin lips curled around the gun barrel making it look almost comical. But Slocum wasn't laughing. "Why are you doing this?"

Ramsey didn't answer. He just waved with his free hand, as if to send Slocum away.

Slocum got to his feet and walked toward the old man. This time, he took the gun out of his mouth, just long enough to shout, "Stay where you are, son."

"I can't do that, Professor."

"I'm no professor."

"Sure you are."

"No, I'm not. That's as phony as everything else about me."

"Don't be silly. You're an actor, and a good one. There's nothing phony in that."

"The hell there isn't. I don't know how to act like a human being, and that's the only acting that really matters. The single most important role of my life was a failure."

"What was that?"

"Father, Slocum. I was a failure as a father. I ruined my daughters' lives. And for what?"

"You didn't ruin anything. Your daughters are fine. They're healthy, beautiful young women."

"And two of them have the morals of a pair of snakes, Slocum. Whose fault is that?"

"Not yours."

"Whose, then?"

"People make their own choices. They have to be responsible."

"You're just making excuses for them. And for me."

Slocum edged a little closer. The gun was still cocked,

and he couldn't afford to spook the old man. But he had to get the gun away from him.

"I'm not making excuses for anybody, Professor. I—"

"Stop calling me that. I told you, I'm a fraud. I'm not a professor of anything." He waved the gun vaguely in Slocum's direction, but it wandered back. Ramsey cradled it now against his cheek. "I'm a fool, Slocum. And you're a fool if you think you can convince me I'm not."

"What about Cordelia?"

"What about her?"

"Don't you think you owe her something?"

"I don't have anything to give her. Just shut up about her."

"You have yourself. Don't you think that matters?"

"I don't think anything matters, Slocum. Not anymore. I lost everything in the fire. Everything except my dignity, and my pride. And I already lost those a long time ago."

"Bullshit, Ramsey."

The old man pointed his chin at Slocum. "That's more like it. Man to man. I like that."

"You're just playing a game now. Why don't you face up to it. You made a couple of mistakes. Big deal! People do that every day."

"Not me."

"Oh, so you're better than everybody else, huh? I thought you said you lost your pride."

"Don't twist my words, Slocum. You can't beat me at my own game."

"You think not?"

"Right. I think not."

"The old man's right, Slocum."

He whirled to find the grinning face of Brett Mackay hovering in the bushes.

24

"You got a long nose, Slocum. Maybe I'll shoot it off for you." Mackay stepped through the bushes, his grin growing wider as he waved the pistol. "Seems like you and me are finally going to finish what we started."

"It's already finished, Mackay."

"You think so, do you? How's about you just ease that pistol out of your holster and drop it on the ground."

Slocum looked at Ramsey, who seemed detached, as if what was happening had nothing to do with him. He reached for his Colt, but Mackay was watching him too closely for him to do anything but comply.

"Use your fingertips, Slocum. Real easy now, just lift it out and let it fall. I even *think* you're trying anything, I'll kill you."

"Like you killed Moseley?"

Mackay laughed. "Yeah. Fancy boy was easy, but I'll bet you a double eagle you won't be no harder. So to speak." He laughed, but he never took his eyes off Slocum's gun hand. "Seems like fancy boys and midgets is all I see these days. Which one are you, Slocum? You a fancy boy? Or just a midget?"

"Where is Marillac?"

"Who?"

"Louis Marillac—the little man who worked with Professor Ramsey?"

"Oh, the shrimp? Huh, that was surprising. Little cuss was tougher than you'd think. Gave me more trouble than that nancy bugger, anyhow. Got to give him credit. Died like a bigger man ought to. Bet you don't have what he had, Slocum, but we'll see."

"I can't believe you give a damn about some theater troupe. Why are you doing this?"

Mackay laughed again, starting to relax. If he had noticed the pistol in Ramsey's hand, he gave no indication. "In the beginning, I done it because the lady paid me to do it. Wanted a little pressure on the old man there. Hell, I like a little free lovin' and it ain't often a man can get *paid* to boot. Like havin' your cake and eatin' it. But you changed all that, Slocum. You had to stick that nose of yours where it didn't belong. That's one thing I never could stand."

Ramsey tried to get to his feet, but Slocum reached out with one hand to hold him down. "Just stay there, Professor."

"That's right, old man. Don't make me shoot you before I'm ready."

"You think you're going to get away with this?" Ramsey said. "You think you can set fire to a man's life and just walk away? Is that what you really think?"

"I think I can do what I want. That's what I think, old man. And that's a fact. You could have made it easy on yourself, and none of this would have happened. If you had taken the hint, sold out like your daughter wanted, you'd be sittin' back east, growing a lot older than you're gonna get now."

"Sheriff Castle knows more than you think he does," Slocum said.

"Ray Castle don't bother me."

As long as Mackay kept talking, there was time. But Slocum couldn't keep him talking forever. Somehow, he had to get his hands on Mackay, or on a gun. He watched Ramsey out of the corner of his eye as the old actor slid his gun, still cocked, under his hip, out of Mackay's line of sight. He winked at Slocum, then said, "You know, Mr. Mackay, it seems to me we can work this out without anyone getting hurt."

"It's too late for that, old man. Way too late. Besides, like I told you, me and Slocum got business that has nothin' to do with you. And there's no way that gets finished without somebody getting hurt. Ain't that right, Slocum?"

"If you say so, Mackay."

"Oh, I do. Pity about the old man. I mean, he ain't got nothing to sell now. Too bad to kill him, but that's life, I guess."

Slocum spotted something beyond Mackay's shoulder, some slight movement in the brush. He tried to watch without letting his eye linger long enough to alert the cowboy. "You know, Brett, you brought most of this on yourself."

Mackay laughed. "Brought what on? Seems to me like you're getting things mixed up, Slocum. It's you that's knee deep in cowshit, and going down fast. Me, I'm doing just fine, thank you very much."

"Pete Harney knows what you've been up to. Seems like some of your friends have been doing a little more talking than they ought to."

"Nobody pays attention to drunken bullshit. And Harney's a windbag. Nobody pays attention to him, either."

"Can you afford to take that chance?"

"Can't afford not to, Slocum. No need to kill Harney, too. Hell, where would a man get a decent drink in this shithole of a town?"

Slocum raised a hand, and Mackay backed away a step. He was skittish, but it enabled Slocum to get a better look at the brush behind him. There was no sign of the movement he'd seen earlier.

"I'm surprised you don't have your usual complement of bullies with you, Mackay."

"Bullies, that what you call them? They're nothing. And I don't need anybody to help me, if that's what you're getting at. Does it look like I need any help, Slocum? For an old man and a busted-up cowboy?"

He saw it again now, a trembling of the bushes as a couple of branches were pushed aside, about halfway through the clump of scrub oaks. A flash of color winked at him, then ducked down out of sight, probably a shirt.

Slocum had to keep Mackay busy without provoking him. He felt as if he were walking barefoot on the edge of a sword. One wrong move and he'd cut himself in half. "Why the fire, Mackay? Why not just run a few people off? Why did you have to kill anybody?"

"Didn't mean that. Not the first one, that fancy fella with his flower water and pretty shirt. But he didn't want to cooperate. When I pushed, I thought he'd run, but the sonofabitch pushed back. Made me look bad. I couldn't let no little frilly boy get away with that."

"So you shot him in the back? That make you look good, did it?"

"It doesn't hardly matter now, does it, Slocum? And that little dwarf. I caught him sneakin' around the cabin. You know about the cabin, don't you, Slocum?"

He didn't wait for an answer. Turning his attention to Ramsey, he said, "Followed your little girl, he did. Wasn't anything I could do about that. Had to shut him up."

Ramsey moved as if to get up, and Mackay snapped a shot in his direction. It spanged through the bushes just behind the old man. "Don't be doing that, now. I won't miss next time."

"Won't be a next time, Brett."

Mackay spun to see who had spoken as Ray Castle stepped through the brush, followed by Pete Harney and Cordelia. "You'd best drop it, Brett. Don't make me kill you, now."

Mackay laughed. "Ray, what'd you want to shoot me for? I ain't done nothing."

"I heard it all, Brett, every last word."

Mackay started to laugh again, then fired twice. One slug caught Castle high on the shoulder. The sheriff spun back, dropping his gun and falling to his knees. Mackay turned toward Slocum, raising the gun as he turned.

Slocum dove for his Colt as the cowboy fired again. He felt his fingers close on the butt of the Navy and he rolled once, swinging the gun around as he came to rest on his belly. Mackay fired again. The bullet dug into the earth so close to Slocum's cheek, he thought he could feel its heat.

Cocking the hammer, Slocum squeezed off a shot as Mackay ran for the brush. He scrambled to his feet, calling for Mackay to stop. He fired again, blindly, and barreled into the undergrowth after the cowboy. He heard hoofbeats as he broke into the open. Mackay had one foot in the stirrups as his horse angled up the far side of the creekbank. Slocum looked for his own horse, and sprinted for him. He jerked the reins free, scattering leaves and broken twigs as he wheeled the chestnut around and dug in his spurs.

He angled across the face of the slope, trying to cut Mackay off. He could see the cowboy ahead of him, lashing at his mount with the reins. Slocum fired again, not expecting to hit anything, but hoping to convince Mackay to pull up. The bullet nicked Mackay's horse and it broke stride. Trying to regain control, the animal stumbled, spilling his rider into the tall grass. Slocum kicked his horse again and the chestnut spurted forward.

Mackay floundered through the waist-high grass as Slocum bore down on him. When he realized he wasn't going to get away, he turned to face his pursuer. He fired again, and Slocum returned it. The slug ripped into Mackay's chest and sent him sprawling. As Slocum reined in, the cowboy got to his knees. He was aiming as Slocum fired his last round.

Mackay fell over backward, his gun tumbling off into the weeds. Slocum charged toward him, but Mackay lay still. His lips moved soundlessly, and a bubble of blood formed on his lips, swelled to the size of a grape, then burst. It trickled down his chin and Slocum saw it drip onto Mackay's open collar.

Dropping to one knee, he reached out to feel for a pulse. There was none. Mackay's eyes reflected the blue sky overhead. Even in death, he still wore the grin.

Shaking his head, Slocum got to his feet. Like a man in a trance, he snatched absently at the reins, then started to walk back downhill, pulling the chestnut after him. It was all so damned pointless.

At the creek, he stopped to scoop up a handful of water. He rinsed his mouth and spat into the clear water. He swallowed the next handful, then stepped into the creek. Wading across, he heard a scream. Letting go of the reins, he raced through the knee-deep stream and charged up the far bank.

Plowing through the green tangle, he swept his arms ahead of him to keep the branches from slashing at his eyes. He broke into the clear to find Cordelia rocking Ramsey's head in her lap. He started toward her, but Harney grabbed him by the arm.

"Let her be, John. There's nothing you can do. He caught a stray from Mackay's gun."

Slocum pulled free and ran to her. He knelt beside her, but she didn't look up. Slocum put a hand on her shoulder and squeezed. She turned toward him for a moment. Tears streamed down her cheeks, and her mouth moved. No sound came out, but he didn't have to hear the question to know what it was. "Why?" Then she turned away.

He didn't know, and he didn't even try to answer. He looked back at Harney, who finished tying a tourniquet on Castle's upper arm. The barkeep waved him over, and Slocum patted Cordelia once more, stroking her hair so full of light and shadow where the sun speared through the trees.

"I got to get Ray back to town, John. He's bleeding pretty bad. Can you take care of the girl?"

"I guess . . . "

25

Slocum traced the long leg with a fingertip. She smiled at him; wriggling a little when it tickled her.

"That's nice," she said.

"It's supposed to be."

"It's good to know that some things do what they're supposed to do."

Slocum didn't answer. Instead, he leaned forward to take a hard nipple between his teeth. He sucked gently, opening his mouth wider for a moment and letting his tongue circle the pebbled aureole. When he pulled away, she followed him. Her hair fell around her shoulders, and he felt it on the back of his neck.

He felt suddenly tired. He rolled onto his side and lay

down. When he sighed, she bent and kissed him on the forehead.

"What's wrong?" she asked.

"I don't know. I guess the last few days have taken something out of me."

She spread her fingers over a large yellow bruise on his chest. "I know what you mean."

"No, I don't think you do."

"Of course I do. But you have to learn to be resilient. Life is hard, but we just have to be harder. If we can do that, we win."

"Not really. You don't beat the worms. They're always there at the end of the road, waiting."

"That's morbid. Don't talk like that, Slocum. Not now. It's not fair. We have a little time. We should use it." She draped a leg over his hips and sat upright, leaning back until her hair slithered over his knees like cool water.

He was aroused in spite of himself, and she raised her hips until he was hard enough, then slowly brought her body down again. He felt the warmth, and she leaned forward, rubbing his chest with open palms. Her hips started to move, slowly at first, each time pausing at the crest, teasing him a moment. The fourth time, he rested his hands on her hips and pulled her down.

"That's more like it," she said, laughing.

He watched the tip of her tongue dart between her lips in time to the movement of her hips. Like a pink serpent's tongue, it flashed at him then vanished, only to reappear a moment later. It was sensual but somehow sinister, as if she were tasting the air, testing it for the presence of something toxic.

He let go of her hips, sliding his hands up along her ribs. He stopped at every bone, counting them with the tips of his thumbs. Below her breasts, he relaxed a little, letting his palms take their weight. He worked the nipples and she leaned toward him. This time, instead of sucking on a breast, he buried his face between them, sliding his hands around her back to pull her toward him.

She let him guide her. He wrapped his arms around her and held on tight. He was conscious of nothing but her body and his own. He stayed hard, but when she tried to move, he slid a hand down over her ass and pressed her hips against him. The sharp bones of her dug into him, and he wanted to cry out with the pain, but it felt too good.

The sun started to come up, leaking into the room like water spurting through a ship's hull. He moved out from under her, and she lay on her back. He watched the orange light splash over her body, filling crevices with shadow. The tangle between her legs glowed with droplets turned to opals by the light; crescents of shade underlined her breasts. Spikes of shadow spilled down over the mounds where her nipples still stood erect.

The light bathed her face. Her eyes glittered, her long lashes caught fire. On her lips, a wavering orange flame trembled as she breathed.

He watched the rise and fall of her breasts, then spread a fan of fingers across her stomach. He moved slowly, as if afraid her skin would sear him, lowering the hand until he could feel the skin on every intake of breath. He rubbed at a few of the tangled curls, watching the little spheres of fire drop out of sight.

She closed a hand over his, pulling him lower, but he stopped when he felt the dampness.

"I don't have much time," she said.

"I know."

"Will you be here when I get back?"

"No."

She said nothing for a long moment. He rested his head on her stomach. He could hear her heart beating steadily. He rode the rise and fall of her breathing like a toy ship on an ebbing tide.

"I guess I understand why," she said. "I wish it could have been different."

Slocum didn't answer. He didn't know quite what to say.

Nothing he could tell her would change anything.

He watched her dress. As the light in the room grew brighter, her skin seemed to take on a glow, as if she were lacquered in gold leaf. As her body slowly disappeared under layers of cloth, he thought of a miser hiding a fortune. When she was dressed, she sat on the edge of the bed.

"Will you come with me to the funeral?"

When he didn't answer, she knew not to press him. "I'd better go. My sisters will be waiting." At the door she stopped for a moment. "Goodbye, Mr. Slocum."

"Goodbye, Portia."

He nodded.

JAKE LOGAN
TODAY'S HOTTEST ACTION WESTERN!